F

and

Joseph

A Make Your Own

Decisions Book!

Book 2: Sharing

by

Natalie

Vellacott

Copyright

Copyright Natalie Vellacott © 2017

ISBN 9781548134211

1.

Reuben is bored. He looks around at the other children in his class. They all seem to be listening to their teacher, Mr Gately, as he teaches them about a country somewhere, a very long way away. Reuben would much rather learn about numbers or even read a book.

He allows his mind to wander and starts thinking about one of the adventures of *The Famous Five*. He loves Enid Blyton books and can't wait to get home so he can start reading another one. He dreams of climbing mountains, exploring caves and sailing across the sea.

The exciting adventures in his mind are suddenly disturbed by a knock on the classroom door. The whole class turns around to see who it is. Mr Gately pauses as he waits for the person to enter. The door opens. A small boy is standing in the doorway.

Everyone stares at the boy wondering whether he has come to the wrong place. He isn't wearing school uniform and he looks really dirty. His clothes are almost like rags and are hanging off his body. He is very thin. His hair hasn't been brushed. The children sitting in the back row hold their noses as become aware of a nasty smell coming from the boy.

"Well, who do we have here?" Mr Gately asks the boy kindly.

"I'm Joseph." The boy sounds scared and a little confused.

"And how old are you Joseph?" Mr Gately wants to find out if the boy is in the right place.

"I'm eight, I think," Joseph manages.

"Is this your first day at school?" Mr Gately looks behind him to see if there is someone with him. Mrs Gibbs, another teacher, appears. She looks flustered.

"Oh, sorry Mr Gately. I was on the phone and Joseph disappeared. I didn't mean for him to interrupt your class. Anyway, now that he is here, he does need to be introduced as he is starting here today. His family have just moved into the area. Now, let's see, his name is Joseph Kline and we think he is eight. I still need to get a few details from his mother so I'm not sure which school he was in before. Can I leave him with you for now?" Mrs Gibbs is closing the door before hearing a response.

"Yes, that's fine. Have a seat over here next to Reuben, Joseph. We can talk a bit more when the lesson has finished." Mr Gately isn't sure whether any of the children will pay attention to his lesson now. He could tell he was already losing them *before* Joseph's arrival.

Joseph walks in and takes the seat next to Reuben as instructed.

1Q. How will Reuben respond to the new arrival?

A. Move his chair slowly away and ignore him completely. <u>*Go to 2.*</u>

B. Smile but then focus on the rest of the lesson. <u>*Go to 3.*</u>

C. Hold his nose because of the smell and look disgusted. <u>*Go to 4.*</u>

D. Offer Joseph a pen, pencil and some paper. <u>*Go to 5.*</u>

2.

Reuben wishes that Mr Gately had sat the new boy somewhere else. He already has his friends Jack and Todd. He doesn't want to have to make friends with someone new. Reuben likes his friendship group and doesn't want new people to be included in it. He decides that if he just ignores Joseph then he will find other people to hang around with. He feels a little guilty but Joseph needs to make the effort to get to know people. Life is difficult sometimes.

Reuben stares ahead at the front board as Mr Gately continues the lesson. He isn't thinking now about mountains and adventures. He is just hoping that the lesson will finish soon so he can get home. He looks across at his friends Jack and Todd who are sitting together on the other side of the classroom. Mr Gately has separated Reuben from them as they don't concentrate in class when they all sit together.

Finally, Reuben breathes a sigh of relief as the end of the lesson arrives. He gets up to walk over to his friends. Jack is already heading towards him. Reuben smiles and stops to talk. He is surprised when Jack doesn't stop but continues walking past him. He wonders if Jack has even seen him. Reuben turns around and sees Jack leaning over and talking quietly to the new boy who had stayed in his seat looking nervous.

2Q. What will Reuben do now?

A. Forget about his friends and go home. Go to 6.

B. Join Jack and Joseph's conversation. Go to 7.

C. Approach Todd instead. Go to 8.

3.

Reuben gives the new boy a big smile. He doesn't want to get into trouble with Mr Gately so he then turns his attention back to his lesson. He tries to listen to the details about the countries in the far off places so that he can actually learn something. He writes the questions that his teacher asks in his exercise book and begins to think about the answers.

Mr Gately asks the children, "Which country is this?" as he points to a map at the front of the room.

Reuben raises his hand, "It's the Philippines, I know because my auntie lives there. She's a missionary......"

"Thankyou Reuben, that's right. It is the Philippines." Mr Gately stops him from going into further detail about the missionary work of his relatives. He knows that Reuben is always keen to talk about it!

After a while, a small voice is heard around the room. "Please Sir, can I have some paper and maybe a pencil?" Joseph waited for a long time hoping that someone might offer them to him so he wouldn't have to bother the teacher.

"Oh, yes, I'm so sorry, Joseph. I thought Reuben would've given them to you. Reuben, it's good that you know the answers to a lot of the questions in class, but you also need to try and think about other people sometimes," Mr Gately reminds Reuben sternly.

Reuben goes a bit red and puts his head down. He decides that he will try to make it up to the new boy Joseph after class. The end of the day finally arrives and Reuben turns to speak to Joseph.

3Q. What will Reuben say to Joseph?

A. *"Hey, I'm sorry about earlier, would you*

like to come back to my house, I'm sure my mum won't mind?" <u>Go to 13.</u>

B. "Can I come to your house?" <u>Go to 14.</u>

C. Nothing, he changes his mind and turns away again. <u>Go to 15.</u>

D. "I will try and bring you some clean clothes and some soap tomorrow." <u>Go to 16.</u>

4.

Reuben is furious that Mr Gately has sent the new boy to sit next to him. He doesn't want anyone that he doesn't know sitting anywhere near him especially not someone who smells as bad as this boy does. He looks at him with disgust and when Joseph tries to smile at him, he turns away and holds his nose.

"REUBEN, HOW DARE YOU BEHAVE LIKE THAT!" The booming voice of Mr Gately thunders from the front of the classroom. I chose the space next to you for Joseph as I thought you would look after him. How would you feel if someone treated you like that on your first day at a new school? I thought you were a Christian as well?!

Definitely not the right way to treat another person whoever they are. Reuben is sent home in disgrace. It will probably take him a long time to learn that he should treat others as he would like to be treated. He must stay in his room. He misses the rest of the adventure and instead stares at a boring wall. Let's start again and make different choices shall we? Go to 1.

5.

Reuben is keen to get to know the new boy to see if they might be friends. He remembers how hard it was when he started a new school and how some of the older children were a bit mean to him. He smiles at Joseph and whispers, "Hi, I'm Reuben." He then pushes a pen, pencil and some paper that he has torn from his notebook towards the new boy.

Joseph smiles at him and says, "Thanks." Then both boys turn back to Mr Gately at the front of the class.

The lesson seems to drag on forever but finally, Mr Gately comes to an end and sends them home for the day.

5Q. What will Reuben say to Joseph?

A. *"Would you like to come back to my house, I'm sure my mum won't mind?" Go to 13.*

B. *"Can I come to your house?" Go to 14.*

C. *Nothing, he's done enough already. Go to 15.*

D. *"I will try and bring you some clean clothes and some soap tomorrow." Go to 16.*

6.

Reuben is hurt and a little angry that Jack would rather talk to Joseph than him. He stares at them for a while then grabs his school-bag and leaves the classroom. He begins walking home on his own. Usually, he would walk with one of his friends, but Jack is obviously busy. Reuben is so angry that he doesn't even bother to look around for his other friend Todd.

He decides to walk a different way home along a country track so that he can get some fresh air and think about things. He prefers to think when he is on his own anyway. He heads for a nearby field belonging to Mr Jack, a local farmer. There is a public footpath running next to the field and Reuben knows it well.

He walks along the footpath and starts to feel a little better from the exercise. He tries to forget about his friends and the new boy. He is nearly at the end of the footpath when he sees something pink through the hedge. The colour catches his eye because everything else is green and brown. He walks quickly to the end of the path and towards a hole in the hedge.

Looking through, he can see a small pink tent arranged in the middle of the grassy area next to the field. Reuben is surprised as he has never seen people camping in the area before and it seems a strange place for the people to have stopped. It is pretty much in the middle of nowhere and quite a long way from other houses and people.

6Q. What will Reuben do?

A. *Spy on the tent for a while to see if anyone is there. Go to 9.*

B. *Go and speak to Mr Jack, the farmer about the tent. Go to 10.*

C. *Lose interest and forget about it. Go to 11.*

D. *Go home and tell his parents. Go to 12.*

7.

Reuben turns back and joins the conversation between Jack and Joseph.

"When is your birthday?" Jack is asking.

"I'm not sure exactly," Joseph answers. "I think sometime in February."

Jack starts to ask, "Why, don't….," and then he stops himself.

Reuben is not as careful and is very curious. "How can you not know your birthday?" he asks.

"I just don't know the date exactly," Joseph mumbles.

"So, where do you live?" Jack changes the subject as Todd walks over and joins them.

"Hi, I'm Todd," he says.

Joseph nods to say hello and then gets up to leave. He seems a bit uncomfortable with everyone coming to talk to him and with all their questions.

7Q. What will Reuben say as Joseph leaves?

A. "Let's all walk home together." Go to 17.

B. Ignore Jack and Todd and ask, "Can I come to your house?" Go to 14.

C. Nothing, he's done enough already. Go to 15.

D. "I will try and bring you some clean clothes and some soap tomorrow." Go to 16.

8.

Reuben feels rejected and looks around for his other friend Todd. All of the children are leaving the classroom. Mr Gately is watching the conversation between Jack and Joseph. He keeps glancing over at Reuben. Reuben can't see Todd anywhere.

Go to 7.

9.

Reuben finds a tree stump to sit on and settles down to watch the tent. He is desperate to know who is camping in this strange place. He knows he really should be getting home because his mum will be worried. He forgets about everything else as he focuses on staring through the hole in the hedge.

Nothing happens for a while and Reuben starts to get a little bored.

Then, he hears a child's voice. "It's Joe mum, look, Joe's back." A little girl who must be about three or four comes out of the tent and runs across the grass.

Reuben can't see where she is going from his position. He leans forward to try and see who the girl is talking about. He falls off the stump and into the bushes. "Yowwwwwl," he yells, as he is stung by a lot of stinging nettles. Then he puts his hand over his mouth as he remembers that he is meant to be spying.

"Who's there?" a woman calls. "Joe, come quick, there's someone in the bushes...."

Reuben hears footsteps moving towards his position.

9Q. What will he do?

A. Scream, "I'm not afraid of you! Haha." <u>Go to 19.</u>

B. Stand up and face the people. <u>Go to 20.</u>

C. Run away. <u>Go to 21.</u>

10.

Reuben is feeling responsible. He knows that this tent is on land belonging to Mr Jack, a local farmer. He checks his watch. He thinks he can get to Mr Jack's house, to report what he has found, within a few minutes. He can ask Mr Jack to phone his mum when he gets there.

He sets off jogging back along the footpath but trips over a stone. He falls down a small bank and into a ditch. He has always been a bit clumsy.

Reuben tries to get up, but his leg hurts and is trapped underneath him. He looks down and sees a bit of blood coming from a cut on his knee. He hates blood and feels very sorry for himself. He starts to cry and doesn't know what to do. He can't see anything apart from the twigs and stones in the ditch. He tries again to get up but he is in too much pain. His only hope is for someone to come along and find him.

He starts shouting, "HELP, I'M TRAPPED IN A DITCH AND MY LEG IS BLEEDING. HELP......!"

Within a few minutes, a voice calls back, "Who is that, where are you?" Reuben recognises the voice but isn't sure who it is.

"I fell into the ditch and I can't get out," Reuben calls back.

A face appears above him. Reuben blinks as he recognises Joseph, the new boy in his class.

"Can I help you out of there?" Joseph offers.

10Q. What will Reuben say?

A. "Go away, I'm praying for someone to come and help me." <u>Go to 22.</u>

B. "Oh, not you! Well, I suppose you can help me." <u>Go to 23.</u>

C. "Oh, hi Joseph, yes please help me!" <u>Go to 24.</u>

D. "What are you doing here?" <u>Go to 25.</u> ·

11.

Reuben decides that going home and reading an adventure book is much more interesting than having a real adventure. He turns away from the tent and walks home. Later he goes to his room and reads a book then falls asleep. This day is the same as every other day in Reuben's life.

What a boring ending Reuben has chosen. Let's start again and see if he can make things more exciting by making different decisions, shall we? <u>Go to 1.</u>

12.

Reuben leaves the tent in the undergrowth and rushes home. He is excited about what he has found and can't wait to tell his mum and dad. He runs up the path leading to his house and opens the door. "Mum, Mum," he calls out. "There's a tent at the edge of one of Mr Jack's fields. Who do you think is there? Can we go and see?"

Dodgy, the family dog, comes running to meet Reuben and licks his hand. Reuben pats him on the head, he loves their pet.

"Oh, hello, Reuben. How was school?" Mrs Sense is used to Reuben's enthusiasm about all sorts of things and decides to ask him about the important thing first.

"Yes, it was fine but Mum, what about this tent?" Reuben wants his mum to really listen to him.

"I expect some people are just passing through and have stopped for the night, Reuben. I tell you what, let's phone Mr Jack and see if he knows anything about it, shall we?" Mrs Sense knows that she will have to do something to stop Reuben going on and on about what he's seen.

"Yes, okay." Reuben wants to know who the people in the tent are. He decides that if his mum tells Mr Jack about the tent, the farmer will probably check it out.

Mrs Sense picks up the phone and dials the number. "Oh hello Mrs Jack, yes we're all okay. I was actually phoning about some campers that

Reuben saw on the way home from school. He thinks they were on your land. Did you know about them?"

Reuben can hear Mrs Jack's reply, "Campers, on our land? No, we haven't had anyone for a few years now. Where exactly were they and how many of them?"

Reuben explains that he has only seen one small tent and gives the directions to it. Mrs Sense passes the information to Mrs Jack.

"I'll tell you what, I'll get my husband to come over to your place. Then, he can collect young Reuben and they can check it out together. Is that okay?" Mrs Jack knows that Reuben is probably desperate to go and investigate.

"Yes, please do that or I won't get a minute's peace!" Mrs Sense laughs

"Right, he'll be over in around thirty minutes I would think. Goodbye then." Mrs Jack hangs up the phone.

"Right, Reuben go and get some boots on and get ready to go," Mrs Sense instructs him.

"Where's Reuben going, I want to go too." Ellie has joined them.

"I'm sure Mr Jack won't mind, but we'd better ask Reuben whether he minds sharing his adventure with you, Ellie," Mrs Sense says carefully.

12Q. What will Reuben decide?

A. Ellie can't go with him. It's his adventure and he wants to enjoy it alone. <u>Go to 26.</u>

B. Ellie can go but she has to let him lead the investigation. <u>Go to 27.</u>

C. Ellie can't go because she's a girl. His brother Toby can go instead. <u>Go to 28.</u>

13.

Reuben feels sorry for Joseph and wants to make him feel like he will fit in at school. He invites him to his house. Joseph looks a bit nervous but agrees to go with Reuben. They set off but Reuben suddenly remembers something. "Don't you need to check with your parents whether it's okay for you to come to my house? Maybe they will worry about you?" he asks.

"No, they won't, it's okay. I told them I would be home later anyway," Joseph says. Reuben sees that he looks away as he says this.

"Okay then." Reuben is surprised by Joseph's answer as they obviously hadn't planned anything. He doesn't want to ask too many questions, though, or to make Joseph feel awkward. He hopes that his mum will sort things out when they get back to his house.

They walk together along the path and then cross the road near Reuben's house. Reuben chats about his books and the things he likes to do; play in the garden, play with Lego, make things and read adventure books. He also tells Joseph that he goes to church on Sundays.

Joseph just listens as Reuben talks. He waits for Reuben to ask him what he likes to do.

Reuben finally pauses for breath and realises that he has been doing all of the talking, "So what do you like doing?" he asks.

"Oh, the same type of things as you....is this your house? WOW!" Joseph seems astonished as they head up the path to the very nice house with a large garden. "These flowers are really beautiful. Is that trampoline yours?!" Joseph sounds as if he can't believe it.

"Yep, come on, let's go in." Reuben opens the door and welcomes his new friend to his home.

"Mum, I've brought a new friend home from school. Is it okay?" Reuben calls.

Dodgy, the family dog, comes running to meet Reuben and licks his hand. He pets him and introduces him to Joseph. Joseph strokes the big dog and Dodgy rolls over on his back.

Mrs Sense appears and looks surprised to see Joseph. She smiles as Reuben introduces him. "It's fine Reuben as long as his mum has given permission."

Reuben looks at Joseph who nods.

Mrs Sense isn't quite satisfied with the silent nod but decides she can look into it later. Joseph definitely needs feeding and could do with a hot bath and a new set of clothes. She feels sorry for him and determines to find out more about him. "Okay then boys, Reuben why don't you go and play and I'll call you when tea's ready. Glad you could join us, Joseph, I'll have to pop by and meet your mum soon. You've just moved to the area have you?"

"Yes, ma'am," Joseph keeps his answers short. He wants to tell the truth as much as possible.

Reuben heads towards the lounge and Joseph follows. Joseph isn't saying much, he seems amazed by all the things he sees.

"These are my Enid Blyton books," Reuben says proudly. "Have you read any *Secret Seven* or *Famous Five* books?"

"Not yet, but I'd like to, can I borrow one?" Joseph asks.

Reuben looks at Joseph with his dirty clothes and hair.

13Q. What will Reuben say?

A. *"Yes, if you have a bath here first."* <u>Go to 29.</u>

B. *"No, I don't lend my books."* <u>Go to 30.</u>

C. *"Yes, but only if I can borrow one of your books as well."* <u>Go to 31.</u>

D. *"Yes, but please look after it as they are my favourite books."* <u>Go to 32.</u>

14.

Reuben forgets his manners and blurts out, "Hey Joseph, can I come to your house?"

Joseph looks shocked and like he doesn't know what to say, "Um, I guess so," he says quietly after a few seconds. "I live nearby."

"Okay, let's go then." Reuben had not intended to invite himself to Joseph's house. He knows it's rude but he just couldn't help himself. Now that it's happened he wants to take the exciting opportunity to check out a new place. He has already memorised his mum's number so he will be able to phone and tell her where he is. He wonders if Joseph's family will have some of his favourite food. He often thinks about food.

The two boys head out of the school together. Mr Gately is pleased that Reuben appears to be befriending Joseph but there is also concern on his face. He heads to the staff office in search of Mrs Gibbs.

Reuben and Joseph walk along the path next to the playground. Reuben chats cheerfully but Joseph is quiet.

After just a few minutes of walking, Joseph suddenly says, "I'm sorry Reuben, I need to go home now and it's probably better if you don't come today. Maybe next time?" Joseph then rushes away before Reuben can respond.

Reuben gazes after him. He feels sad that he

won't be able to go to Joseph's house but also very curious about him. Joseph seems to have headed straight towards land belonging to the farmer, Mr Jack. There are no houses in that area, as far as Reuben knows.

14Q. What will Reuben do?

A. Go home and speak to his mum about Joseph.. Go to 33.

B. Climb a tree and look around. Go to 34.

C. Follow Joseph. Go to 35.

D. Pray about what to do. Go to 36.

15.

Reuben turns his back on Joseph and starts walking out of the classroom. Mr Gately walks past and says, "Reuben, can you come with me for a second, please?"

"Okay." Reuben isn't sure why his teacher would want to speak with him but he knows he must go with him. He follows Mr Gately to his office.

"Reuben, I'm not sure how long Joseph will be with us but I really hope you can make an effort to look after him. I'm counting on you because I know that you are a Christian. That's right, isn't it?" Mr Gately asks the question although he already knows the answer.

"Yes, I'm a Christian," Reuben admits. He knows that Mr Gately is trying to remind him that he should try to be a good friend to Joseph because of his faith.

15Q. What will Reuben do now?

A. Ask for someone else to be Joseph's friend. Go to 37.

B. Go back and look for Joseph. Go to 38.

C. Pray that he will be able to help Joseph. Go to 39.

D. Refuse to do what Mr Gately says. Go to 40.

16.

Reuben wants everyone, including his teacher, to see how generous and kind he is. He says loudly to Joseph, "I'll bring you some soap and clothes tomorrow." Everyone stops talking and turns to stare at Reuben and Joseph.

Mr Gately looks upset and comes rushing over. "Reuben, I'm sure you are trying to be helpful, but that's really not the way to go about it."

Joseph looks stunned. He freezes for a few seconds before turning and rushing out of the classroom.

"Wait, Joseph." Mr Gately follows him outside but by the time he gets there Joseph has gone.

Reuben goes home. He is greeted enthusiastically by Dodgy, the big family dog. He licks his hand as he enters the front door. Reuben pets him and feels slightly better.

He still feels bad and can't understand why Joseph left the classroom so quickly. He is just trying to be practical. Joseph obviously needs soap for a bath and some new clothes. Reuben has more than enough of his own and had thought he could share with Joseph. He knows that the Bible says to help those in need and to share with others. This is what he is trying to do!

Reuben takes the promised items to school the next day after asking his mum for them. Mrs Sense raises her eyebrows when Reuben tells her what happened but she doesn't say anything for the time being.

Joseph isn't at school the next day or the day after. In fact, Joseph doesn't come back to school and Reuben doesn't see him again.

Mrs Sense sits down with Reuben to talk things through. She carefully explains how Joseph probably felt when Reuben offered him the things in front of his whole class. "Why did you say it so loudly if he was just next to you, Reuben?" she asks.

"I don't know," Reuben says quietly.

"I think you do Reuben," Mrs Sense prompts him.

Reuben feels uncomfortable as he thinks

back. "Probably because I wanted people to see that I was generous."

"I think that's right," Mrs Sense says. "Do you think God wants us to show off when we have a lot of things or make a fuss out of giving things to others? How do you think you would have felt if you were Joseph?"

Reuben feels terrible and knows that what he did was wrong. "Oh Mum, I hope Joseph is okay?"

"We can pray for him Reuben, I'm sure it wasn't just what you said that made him run away. I heard that his family have a lot of difficulties at the moment," Mrs Sense tries to make her son feel a little better.

Reuben has learned an important but painful lesson. If he wants to try and behave differently towards Joseph to see what happens, he will need to start the book again and make different decisions. Go to 1.

17.

Reuben doesn't realise that their attention is worrying Joseph. "Let's all walk home together," he says. He is pleased with himself for having the idea and thinks that he is helping Joseph to settle in at school.

"Yes, great idea," Jack and Todd respond together. They have recently been allowed to start walking to school by themselves. Reuben was the first to be allowed due to being one of the oldest in his class. He is nearly nine now and a good six months older than his friends.

"Okay, I guess," Joseph mumbles. He feels that he doesn't really have a choice because Reuben is so enthusiastic about the idea. Reuben is already looking over towards Mr Gately to make sure he has seen his generous offer to the new boy.

The four boys head out of school together and start walking down the pathway next to their playground. They chat to each other. Joseph is quite quiet though and gives short answers to their questions.

"Where do you live then?" Jack asks.

"Just over that way," Joseph is vague and points in a random direction. "We can go to your houses first. I think mine is furthest away."

Reuben is surprised as he doesn't remember telling Joseph where he lives. He assumes that one of the others must've mentioned it.

They walk to Jack's house. He waves a cheerful goodbye and heads up his pathway. "Wow, is this Jack's house? It's really big. How many families live here?" Joseph asks.

"Just Jack's family, I think," Reuben replies. Reuben is surprised by Joseph's question. He always thought that Jack had a small house, at least it is a lot smaller than his.

They reach Todd's house next and Todd also

disappears after waving goodbye. "Do they have their own rooms?" Joseph asks.

"Of course." Reuben doesn't know what to say. He really wants to see Joseph's house now but senses that Joseph isn't ready for guests.

"Right, here's my house." Reuben marches proudly up to the door. "See you tomorrow," he says. He leaves Joseph standing in the street outside. He rushes into the house and then to a window. He peers out from behind a curtain and can see Joseph still standing gazing up at his house.

17Q. What will he do?

A. Wait until he leaves and then try to follow him. Go to 35.

B. Gather some books and toys that he doesn't want and give them to Joseph at school. Go to 42.

C. Ask his mum if Joseph can come in. Go to 43.

D. Forget about Joseph and focus on his birthday party plans. Go to 44.

19.

Reuben decides that being loud and weird might actually scare the people away from him. He jumps up, rubs his stung leg, then shouts,

"I'm not afraid of you, haha!" Then he falls back over as he trips over the stump. He lands in a heap on the ground.

It looks like his tactic has failed. The people are still coming towards him. What will he do instead? *Go back to 9Q.*

20.

Reuben accepts that he has been caught spying. He stands up and brushes off his school uniform. He tries to ignore the nettle stings which are really very painful.

A lady who looks a little older than Reuben's mum is staring at him through the hole in the hedge. "Who are you and why are you watching us?" she asks.

Reuben can see that she looks dirty and is wearing clothes that have holes. He can't see the little girl anymore but can hear her chattering away.

"It's okay Mum, I'll sort this out, it's just a boy who goes to my school." The new boy from Reuben's school, Joseph, appears next to Reuben. He must've walked around the hedge when he first heard Reuben yell. Reuben is now face to face with him. "So, why were you spying on my mum and sister?" Joseph asks.

"Um, um, I don't know. I just saw the tent there and wondered who was staying in it,"

Reuben responds.

"Why didn't you just talk to them and find out?" Joseph says sensibly.

"I was afraid and I'm not meant to talk to strangers." Reuben knows that he is also not meant to spy on people but he doesn't mention this. "Why are your family staying in a tent, anyway?" Reuben has recovered himself and finds his curiosity returning.

Now, it's Joseph's turn to feel awkward. "We're just staying here for a bit, that's all, until our house gets sorted out," he explains.

"So, that's why you are so dirty, I suppose?"

"Yes, but it's just for a while."

Reuben knows that he should at least try to help Joseph but the whole situation is a big one for an eight-year-old. He wishes his mum was with him.

20Q. What will he say?

A. *"That sounds fun, camping in the fields! I'm going to ask if I can join you."* <u>Go to 45.</u>

B. *"I'm sure my church will help you if we ask them."* <u>Go to 46.</u>

C. *"Do you mind if I tell my parents that you are here?"* <u>Go to 47.</u>

21.

Reuben jumps up and starts to run as fast as he can go. He heads back along the path towards his school. His legs are stinging from the nettles but he tries to ignore the pain.

He hears footsteps running behind him and looks around quickly. Someone is chasing him!

"Hey, stop!" the person shouts. Reuben recognises the voice but isn't sure who it is. Whoever it is is very fast, though, and Reuben has never been a quick runner. He looks back again and trips over a tree branch in his path. He goes flying and tumbles into a ditch next to the path. His school bag sails over his head and lands a few metres away. Now, he has a cut knee, a lot of stings and he is stuck in a ditch. He is also pretty dirty. He wants to cry but fear keeps him silent as the person that had been chasing him arrives.

He looks up and blinks. It's Joseph, the new boy at school.

"What, what, are you doing here?" Reuben stammers.

"I could ask you the same question. Why did you run away?" Joseph asks. "I saw you spying on some people in a tent. Why were you doing that? Do you know them?"

"No, I just saw them there and was curious," Reuben answers.

"I saw them as well on my way home from school," Joseph says.

"I think you need to go home now Reuben, you need to get that cut cleaned." Joseph points to Reuben's knee which is trickling a small amount of blood down his leg. "Do you need some help getting out of there?"

21Q. What will Reuben do or say?

A. Accept the offer of help. <u>Go to 24.</u>

B. Say to Joseph,"Don't you know the people in the tent?" <u>Go to 49.</u>

C. Say to Joseph,"Please leave me alone. I can sort myself out." <u>Go to 50.</u>

22.

Hmm, if Reuben really is praying for someone to come and help him can he really reject Joseph like this. He thinks of a story that his dad had told him once about a man in the middle of a lake in a boat that is sinking. The man is praying for God to send someone to rescue him. Someone offers to help him swim to the riverbank. Someone throws him a life raft. Someone else offers to call a lifeguard. The man says "No, thankyou, I'm waiting for God to rescue me." The man drowns.

The story isn't true but God sometimes uses other people to help us when we are in trouble. We need to accept their help. Maybe Reuben should consider that God might have sent Joseph to help him. Does it really matter who it is as long as he gets out of the ditch? *Go back to 10Q and try a different option.*

23.

Reuben starts with, "Oh, not you!"

Before he can say anything else, Joseph responds, "Okay, then. I'll leave you to it. Have fun getting out of the ditch. Bye Reuben." Joseph walks away.

Reuben is still stuck in the ditch and his leg is still bleeding. He asks God to help him but he has a strange feeling that God has already sent someone to help him but that he has rejected the help. He regrets his foolishness.

Shall we see if Reuben can be nicer to Joseph when he arrives? *Go back to 10Q.*

24.

Joseph helps Reuben to get up and looks at his injuries. Reuben is in pain but just wants to get home.

"Thanks for helping me," he says. "Maybe we can walk home together?"

"Yes, okay. Let's go," Joseph says.

The two boys walk out of the field and head

towards Reuben's house. Reuben limps due to his cut knee but is glad to be getting home.

They arrive and Joseph stares up at the big house, "Wow, is this really your house?"

"Yes, do you like it?" Reuben asks him.

"It's amazing!" Joseph continues to stare as if needing time to take it all in.

Reuben heads up the path towards his house. He waves goodbye to Joseph who comments that he lives further along in the village.

Reuben is suspicious. There is something not quite right about Joseph. He forgets about his injured knee and rushes into his house. He goes straight to a window so that he can watch Joseph from behind a curtain. He expects that Joseph will leave straight away but by the time he gets to the window, Joseph is still standing in the street and staring at the house.

Mrs Sense thinks she hears Reuben arriving home but she is busy doing something.

24Q. What will Reuben do?

A. Ask his mum if he can invite Joseph in. <u>Go to 48.</u>

B. Run outside and shout "My house is bigger than yours, haha!" <u>Go to 53.</u>

C. Follow Joseph back to his house. <u>Go to 35.</u>

D. Forget about Joseph and start planning his birthday party. <u>Go to 44.</u>

25.

"That doesn't matter," Joseph replies after Reuben questions him. "Do you want my help or not?"

Joseph obviously doesn't want to talk about this. Reuben needs to decide whether or not he wants to be helped! *Go back to 10Q.*

26.

Reuben looks at his little sister standing keenly waiting.

"No, she can't go. I want to do this by myself and I was the one who found the tent," Reuben says.

Ellie looks so disappointed and then bursts into tears.

"Ellie, please stop that. There will be another time. Why don't you go and watch a DVD with Toby?" Mrs Sense wants to distract Ellie quickly.

Ellie continues sobbing but wanders towards the living room to find a DVD.

Mrs Sense turns to Reuben. "That's a real shame, Reuben. Ellie would have loved to have come with you. Perhaps you should think about other people a little more in future."

"But Mum, I really, really want to have an adventure by myself," Reuben insists.

"Yes, I know Reuben, but we can't always have what we want and you need to be kind to your sister. How would you feel if she had found something exciting but refused to let you join her? Actually, I think she tends to let you join her games a lot of the time, doesn't she?" Mrs Sense wants Reuben to think again but she's not going to force him.

There is a knock at the door. Mr Jack has arrived.

26Q. What will Reuben do?

A. Leave without Ellie. <u>Go to 54.</u>
B. Take Ellie with him. <u>Go to 55.</u>

27.

Reuben looks at his little sister Ellie, keenly waiting for his reply. He really wanted to have the adventure by himself but knows that Ellie will be disappointed.

"Yes, okay, you can come as well Ellie. You have to let me go first though if we find things, okay?" Reuben bargains with Ellie.

"Yes, yes, okay. I will follow you," Ellie says.

"Thankyou, Reuben, that is very generous

and kind," Mrs Sense says.

There is a knock at the door. Mr Jack has arrived.

Go to 55.

28.

Reuben looks at his little sister Ellie waiting keenly. He is annoyed.

"Ellie can't come. She's a girl. Let's get Toby instead," he says.

Ellie bursts into tears and runs from the room.

Mrs Sense is amazed. "Reuben that was really cruel. Toby is too young to go with you and isn't even here. Why would you hurt your sister like that?"

"I just thought it should be a boys only thing," Reuben explains.

"You saw how much you hurt Ellie, what are you going to do now?" Mrs Sense is firm.

"I guess I should say sorry," Reuben says. He doesn't sound very sorry and marches off to find Ellie. Ellie has run out into the garden and is hiding somewhere crying. Reuben searches for her for a while but can't find her. Finally, he goes back into the house.

"I'm afraid Mr Jack came while you were in the garden Reuben. I decided that due to your bad behaviour you're not allowed to go with him today. I'd like you to think about how your behaviour affects other people." Mrs Sense is upset, she had hoped that she wouldn't see behaviour like this from Reuben at his age.

Now, it is Reuben's turn to cry and run upstairs to his room. He has missed out on an adventure. Perhaps he should start the book again and make better decisions next time. Go to 1.

29.

Reuben decides that he will only lend his books to Joseph once he has cleaned up a bit. He knows that things are not as important as people but he just loves his books so much and can't bear to think of them getting ruined. Besides, he feels that he is being pretty generous in making the offer to lend his books. Joseph would just be doing his bit by cleaning up first.

Turning to Joseph he says, "Yes, of course you can borrow them one at a time.....but you will need to have a bath first."

Joseph's face falls and he looks as if he is about to cry. He drops the book he had been looking at on the floor and backs away from it. "You know Reuben, my mum is probably wondering where I am, I should get home." Joseph rushes back towards the front door, opens it and starts to leave.

Mrs Sense hears the noise and comes out of the kitchen. "Leaving so soon Joseph? Are you okay?" she sounds concerned.

"Yes thankyou, I just need to get home." Joseph runs down the drive.

"Reuben, what happened? I thought you were showing Joseph around and that he was going to stay for tea?" Mrs Sense is confused now.

"I don't know Mum, he asked to borrow a book but then he dropped it on the floor and ran off." Reuben avoids telling his mum exactly what happened.

"Did you tell him that he could borrow the book?"Mrs Sense wants to get to the bottom of this quickly.

"Yes, um…," Reuben hesitates.

Mrs Sense knows that there is more to the story. She can tell by Reuben's responses. "Reuben, what else did you say to him?"

"I said he could borrow my books, one at a time, if he had a bath first," Reuben says. "What's wrong with that Mum? I don't want my books to get ruined and I thought I was being nice by letting him borrow them."

"Oh, Reuben, you have a lot to learn." Mrs Sense shakes her head. "The best thing to do is to put yourself in Joseph's place. Think of how you would feel if you were poor and didn't have a lot of things. Then you are invited to go to your friend's house. The friend seems to have everything that you don't have and seems to be very rich. You wish things could be different. You just want to borrow one small thing from your friend because you know they have more than enough. Then your friend reminds you that you are poor and they are rich. Do you think you would still want to borrow the thing or stay in your friend's house?" Mrs Sense hopes Reuben understands.

"But I didn't tell him that he is poor. I don't even know if he is!" Reuben protests.

"Why do you think he is so dirty and his clothes like rags?" Mrs Sense says. "Of course he is poor and by telling him to have a bath you are reminding him that the two of you are from different worlds and that you can never really be proper friends. It's going to be very hard for you to sort this out, Reuben." Mrs Sense feels sad as she knows that Reuben didn't intend to hurt Joseph.

29Q. What will Reuben do about this?

A. Invite Joseph to his birthday party. Go to 56.

B. Give up—some friendships are just too difficult. Go to 57.

C. Try to find out where Joseph lives and pay him a visit at home. Go to 58.

D. *Pray that God will help him decide what*

to do. <u>Go to 59.</u>

30.

"No, these are my books!" Reuben snatches the book away from Joseph.

"Why did you show them to me?" Joseph looks like he might cry.

"So you could see all the things I have," Reuben says.

"I think I want to go home now. Bye Reuben." Joseph rushes towards the front door of the house.

Oh, that was pretty selfish of Reuben. Surely it wouldn't have cost him that much to lend one of his books to his new friend who doesn't seem to have anything? How does God feel about Reuben's behaviour? Reuben has also missed the chance to show Joseph that he cares about him. Joseph may have become a good friend of Reuben's but not now! Reuben needs to spend some time thinking about this and if he wants to change his attitude then he will need to start the book again! <u>Go to 1.</u>

31.

Reuben loves reading and sees an opportunity to get some more books. He thinks it is fair that if he lends his books to Joseph he should get something in return.

"Tell you what, let's swap books. You can give me one of yours at school tomorrow…," Reuben says smiling.

"Um, okay, well, I don't think I can find any of my books right now. They are still in boxes as we've only just moved." Joseph hopes he sounds believable.

"Let's wait then until you have a book to swap," Reuben says. "Or your mum could buy you a book so we can swap. I can tell you where she can buy these books if you want." Reuben thinks he is being helpful and doesn't notice the look on Joseph's face.

"Okay, maybe we can talk about this next time. Actually, I think I have to go now anyway," Joseph says as he begins heading towards the front door.

"But I thought you were going to eat with us?" Reuben calls.

"Next time, have to go," Joseph says as he dashes out of the door and down the pathway.

Mrs Sense appears. "Reuben, what happened? I thought Joseph was staying for tea?"

"I don't know, he left when I suggested we swap books." Reuben is really confused.

"Oh Reuben, do you think Joseph has any books for you to borrow? I think his family is probably quite poor. and he doesn't have many things of his own. Didn't you see his dirty clothes?" Mrs Sense explains. "I hope he isn't upset now."

Reuben hadn't even thought of this and feels quite guilty. He realises that he was being pretty selfish in trying to get something for himself rather than giving to his new friend freely.

Go to 29Q

32.

It's a hard thing for Reuben to do as he loves his books and really doesn't want to see them lost or damaged. However, he knows that his friendship with Joseph is more important than his books. He also realises that he has plenty of books and more than enough to share.

"Yes, you can borrow that one and take the second one as well so that when you finish you can move straight on. Please be careful with them though. I love reading and would like to read them again soon." Reuben feels good as he sees Joseph's face light up.

Joseph holds the two books as if they are very special and important to him.

"Do you think your mum might have a plastic bag or something I could put them in so they don't get dirty?" Joseph asks.

Reuben is pleased. He had been bothered by Joseph's dirty clothes and thought that his books might get dirty. "Yes, I'm sure we have one around."

"Reuben, tea time….," Mrs Sense calls the boys. "Wash your hands first please."

They sit up at the table and Mrs Sense puts plates of food in front of them. Joseph looks at Reuben who says, "We need to thank God first." Reuben says a short prayer and adds amen at the end.

Joseph starts eating quickly, very quickly, and doesn't stop until his plate is completely empty. Reuben's still half-way through this food.

"Oh, Joseph, you are a growing boy. Have some more chicken." Mrs Sense piles more of the dish onto his plate hoping to get some flesh onto his bones. He is so thin!

"Thankyou, thankyou so much." Joseph truly seems very grateful and Mrs Sense wonders when it was that he last had a good meal.

They finish off their food and Joseph says that he needs to leave. He picks up the plastic bag with the two books and heads for the door. He is carrying the bag carefully. He says goodbye as he leaves.

32Q. *What will Reuben say?*

A. "Can I come and see your house now?" <u>Go to 60.</u>

B. "See you at school tomorrow." <u>Go to 61.</u>

33.

Reuben heads home. He is disappointed that he didn't get the chance to check out Joseph's house. He was hoping he might have some cool toys or books that they could play with or read.

He reaches his house and his mum answers the door. "How was school, Reuben?" she says.

Dodgy, the family dog, comes running to meet Reuben and licks his hand. He pets him and Dodgy rolls over on his back.

"Okay Mum, there was a new boy, Joseph. He looked quite dirty though and he didn't have any uniform or even a bag!" Reuben says.

Mrs Sense's eyebrows are raised, "Oh, really? I wonder where his family live. Did he tell you?"

"Not really, I was going to go and see his house but then he changed his mind on the way home from school," Reuben says.

"I hope he actually invited you, Reuben, and

that you didn't just invite yourself again." Mrs Sense knows Reuben only too well.

"Um, well," Reuben says.

"Reuben, we have spoken about this before. You can't just invite yourself to someone else's house. It's very rude. And, this was a new boy who you didn't even know! That could also be dangerous..... What are we going to do with you?" Mrs Sense hopes that one day Reuben will listen to the things she tries to teach him.

"I wanted to see Joseph's house in case he had some new toys or books that I haven't seen before," Reuben continues.

"Reuben, is that really a good reason for making friends with a new boy, do you think?" Mrs Sense is shocked by Reuben's comment.

"No, I suppose not." Reuben realises how bad it sounds, but at least he is being truthful. He is still very curious about Joseph.

"I think I will phone your school and find out what the teachers know about this boy if he's just started," Mrs Sense says.

33Q. What will Reuben say?

A. No, don't do that mum, I don't want to talk to him again anyway. Go to 62.

B. Yes, that's a good idea. Go to 63.

34.

Reuben looks around and sees a tall tree with lots of big branches. He drops his school bag on the ground and climbs it as quickly as he can. He perches on a branch and looks through the leaves. He can see the back of Joseph as he walks away from where they had stopped.

That wasn't the best thing for Reuben to do, was it? He is now up a tree when he could have been following Joseph. What can he do while he is up a tree!?

34Q. What will Reuben do?

A. Get down from the tree and follow Joseph. Go to 35.

B. Climb another tree nearer to where Joseph was heading. Go to 64.

35.

Reuben tries to follow Joseph but he has already disappeared. Reuben heads in the direction he thinks Joseph has gone. He feels like a detective as he keeps his distance. He hides behind trees as they enter a wooded area and tries to make sure he is very quiet. He catches sight of Joseph slightly ahead of him. After a while, he can also see something pink through the trees. He carries on walking and sees that Joseph is heading directly for the large pink thing. It looks like it could be a tent.

Reuben loses sight of Joseph for a few seconds. He ducks behind another tree to make sure he is not seen. *Where on earth did Joseph go?* Reuben wonders. *How could he have just disappeared when I was watching him?*

He doesn't have that much time to think about it as suddenly a hand grabs his shoulder from behind.

"Why are you following me, Reuben?" Joseph asks him.

"Well, I....." Reuben has been caught red-handed and doesn't know what to say. "If you are going home then why are you walking into the woods leading to the fields. There are no houses there."

"Why do you even care?" Joseph doesn't sound angry, just sad.

"I'm not sure, where are you going though?" Reuben finds his tongue and his curious nature returns.

"Okay, I guess I'll have to tell you, although I don't think my mum will be that happy. Let's go then." Joseph begins walking again and indicates that Reuben should follow him.

35Q. *What will Reuben do?*

A. Decide that he really should get home. <u>Go to 65.</u>

B. Follow Joseph. <u>Go to 66.</u>

36.

Reuben closes his eyes and offers a quick prayer to God. He asks God for help as he really doesn't know what to do. After he has finished praying he remembers that Joseph has already told him that he can't go to his house today. He feels that God wants him to be patient. Reuben decides to go to his own house.

<u>Go to 33.</u>

37.

Reuben really feels as if he's done enough already and he doesn't want to share his friends with the new boy. He also decides that he is probably more intelligent than Joseph and he knows he is definitely from a better family. Reuben doesn't want to refuse to do what his teacher is asking directly so he comes up with another idea.

"I think it might be better for Daniel to look after him, Sir." Reuben tries to look as if he really believes this and has thought about it a lot.

"Oh, really? Why do you think that?" Mr Gately is disappointed but wants to hear Reuben's reason before making a judgement.

"Well, because he looks like he is more Daniel's type of person and Daniel doesn't have many friends," Reuben suggests.

"What do you mean, 'Daniel's type of person,' Reuben?" Mr Gately is annoyed. He knows that Reuben is just making up reasons to try to avoid the friendship.

"Well, he probably lives in the same area of the village as Daniel and..." Reuben doesn't know how to explain himself other than just to say it, "....you know, the cheap and poor part."

"Oh, Reuben, I'm so sad to hear you say something like that. What if you were poor or had been born to parents who lived in the cheap area? Do you think that would make you less intelligent? Do you think you would be happy not to have any friends?" Mr Gately looks at him over the top of his glasses.

Reuben looks down. He feels guilty but he really doesn't want the burden of a new friend at the moment.

"Very well, I'm not going to ask Daniel to

befriend Joseph because he may not be with us much longer. His parents are probably moving out of the area as they can't afford to live here anymore. I suppose that doesn't bother you, Reuben, as Daniel wasn't one of your friends anyway." Mr Gately really wants Reuben to learn a lesson but he isn't going to force him.

"I think I'll ask Jack to help with Joseph instead. I saw him talking to Joseph today and I know he is a kind boy," Mr Gately continues.

"But, Jack's one of my close friends," Reuben protests.

"I know that," Mr Gately tells him. "Right, thankyou for coming to see me. You'd best get home now Reuben."

Reuben wanders out of the classroom and heads home. He walks on his own as his friends have left already. He also notices that Joseph has gone.

The next day in school, the first thing Reuben sees is that Jack and Joseph are sitting together. Todd, Reuben's other close friend, is now sitting next to Daniel! There is no one sitting next to Reuben anymore.

He looks over and sees Jack whispering something to Joseph. They both laugh about it. Joseph looks a little bit cleaner today and is wearing school uniform. He still looks quite scruffy and needs to comb his hair. The students at the back of the class are no longer holding their noses. Joseph has obviously had a bath.

Reuben looks in the other direction and sees Todd passing a piece of paper to Daniel. Daniel looks surprised but his eyes light up as he reads it. He smiles at Todd. Reuben feels very jealous. What has happened? Both of his friends now seem to have other friends! What if they don't need him anymore?

Mr Gately joins the class. "Morning children, you will probably have noticed the new seating arrangements. I felt it was time for a change. Reuben, you will have to wait for the next new person to join us before you have a partner again. I hope it won't be too long." Mr Gately turns his attention to the lesson. Reuben feels his face going red. Everyone must know that he has rejected Joseph as a friend.

Maths is one of Reuben's favourite subjects. He tries to forget what has happened and focus on the lesson. Mr Gately is asking a question. Reuben raises his hand.

"Joseph, yes, please give us your answer." Reuben is shocked. He is usually the first one to give the answers in maths and, most of the time, Mr Gately chooses Reuben first.

"Seventy- six," Joseph says quietly.

"Correct, thankyou," the teacher responds.

This pattern continues throughout the lesson.

When Reuben is finally chosen, he gets the answer wrong as he was focusing too much on beating Joseph. Even Daniel, who never says anything in class, answers one question correctly. He seems to have slightly more confidence now that Todd is paying attention to him.

At the end of the day, Reuben can't wait to get home and sulk. He seems to have lost his closest friends and he knows it is his own fault.

He gets up to leave the classroom.

Todd calls out, "Wait, hey, Reuben, wait. Would you like to come back to my place later? I've invited Daniel as well as he's never been to my house."

37Q. What will Reuben say?

A. *Yes, I'd like that. <u>Go to 67.</u>*

B. *Only if Daniel doesn't come. <u>Go to 68.</u>*

C. *No, sorry, I have homework to do. <u>Go to 69.</u>*

38.

"Okay, Mr Gately, please can I go straight away as I might be able to catch him before he leaves," Reuben says.

"Thankyou Reuben. I think he could do with

a friend. Just please be a little bit careful when you talk to him. I don't want him being upset by awkward questions," Mr Gately reminds him.

"Yes, Mr Gately, I understand." Reuben rushes back to try and find Joseph. He walks into an almost empty classroom and sees Joseph fiddling around near Mr Gately's desk.

"Hey, Joseph. What are you doing?" Reuben asks.

Joseph jumps away from the desk and hides his hands behind his back. "Oh, nothing, I was just looking around to see what's in the classroom," he says.   .

38Q. What will Reuben say?

A. *What's in your hands?* <u>*Go to 70.*</u>
B. *Shall we walk home?* <u>*Go to 71.*</u>

39.

Reuben listens to his teacher and says a quick prayer to God. He knows that it is always good to pray about things and that God always hears.

In this case, though, Reuben already knows how he should behave towards other people as he has read about it in his Bible. Reuben knows that

he needs to befriend Joseph and try to help him.
He is reminded of this as he prays.
Go to 38.

40.

"No, I don't care about Joseph and I'm not going to be his friend," Reuben answers.

Mr Gately is shocked. He had at least thought that Reuben would properly consider his request.

"I don't like poor people and Joseph smells. He also won't have any toys or games I can play with. There is nothing for me in the friendship. I already have my friends. We are not like Joseph," Reuben continues.

"I think I've heard enough of this. Reuben, it's clear that you need to change your attitude. Not only to Joseph but to all those around you. Is this what your parents taught you at home or something you read in the Bible?....Actually, I know it's neither." Mr Gately is very upset and angry.

"I'm going to get your mum to come and collect you so that I don't have to look at you in class again today," Mr Gately finishes. He sits down and puts his head in his hands as he dials Reuben's home number.

Oh! What was Reuben thinking? He should never speak to a teacher like that! There is no way for him to sort this out. If he wants to know what happens in this story. He will have to start the book again with a change of attitude. <u>Go to 1.</u>

41.

On arriving back at the house, Dodgy greets the new arrivals cheerfully and slobbers all over them. Mrs Sense pulls him away as she knows he will just carry on otherwise.

Mrs Sense does her best to make some extra space and settle them in. She puts Joseph in Reuben's room and Ellie shares with Jessica. Mrs Kline is given a sofa bed downstairs. She seems grateful to have the chance to rest properly.

Mr Sense arrives home later and the families have dinner together. The Sense's don't want to ask too many questions before Mrs Kline is ready to talk so they concentrate on making her feel at home.

"Oh, you have some great books," Mrs Kline comments as she looks around. "This is a really big house!"

"God has blessed us a lot," Mrs Sense answers. She notices that Mrs Kline looks down when she mentions God.

"I'm really tired now, would it be okay if we all went to bed early tonight?" Mrs Kline asks.

"Yes, please do whatever you feel like doing and when you need anything just help yourself or ask if you are unsure." Mrs Sense wants to make them feel relaxed.

Later, the families are sleeping peacefully. Dodgy gets up and pads across the kitchen. He can hear a noise near the back door. He growls, a low sound deep in his throat. He can see a figure at the door and he doesn't know who they are or what they are doing making noises in the middle of the night.

There is a smash as the door glass breaks. The figure puts its hand through the hole and opens the door. He moves into the kitchen. Dodgy pounces growling and barking. The big dog sinks his teeth into the leg of the man who yells, "YOOOOWWWWL. YOU STUPID DOG. GET OFF ME!"

Lights go on upstairs and people start rushing around. "What's going on, Mum? Dad?" The children are afraid.

"Wait here everyone, I'm going to see what Dodgy is doing. It's probably nothing. Maybe one of his doggy dreams again." Mr Sense tries not to scare them.

He grabs a heavy book and heads slowly

downstairs. Mrs Kline is already there and is looking towards the kitchen where a man is still yelling, "HEY, GET THIS DOG OFF ME!"

"Wait, I recognise that voice, but no, it can't be." Mrs Kline follows behind Mr Sense as he walks towards the kitchen and switches on the light.

A man is lying on the floor, Dodgy is on top of him and still has his teeth in the man's leg. "Good dog, very good dog," Mr Sense tells the dog.

"Oh no!" Mrs Kline sees the face of the intruder. "Patrick!? What are you doing here? Surely, you haven't turned to burglary now as well? I was hoping so much that the fraud was a one off...," she starts crying.

"You know this man?" Mr Sense looks at her sharply. "Dodgy, heel." The dog looks confused but lets go and obeys.

The man starts rubbing his leg as he looks up at them.

"Yes, it's my husband, Patrick and it's a long story," Mrs Kline says. All of the others have by now gathered in the doorway.

"Dad?" Joseph says. "Is it really you?"

"I'm so sorry, I didn't want to disturb all of you and I needed to check that my family was really here," Mr Kline explains.

"So, you weren't trying to burgle us?" Mr Sense can't make sense of this.

"Of course not, I came looking for my family," Mr Kline says, as if it's perfectly reasonable for him to have broken into the house at night!

"Why not knock on the door like a normal person?" Mrs Sense asks as she rubs her face sleepily. "Here, put this on the bite and we'll get some more treatment for it tomorrow." She hands him some cream and a bandage.

"I didn't know if they wanted to see me. I was afraid someone might shut the door in my face. I thought if I broke in then it might be easier to talk to them." Mr Kline stops as he realises how crazy his plan sounds.

"You do realise that I might have hit you with this?" Mr Sense shows him the heavy book. "It could've done some serious damage. Look, it's the middle of the night and we all need to get back to sleep, can we try and sort this out in the morning do you think?"

"Yes, I'm so sorry about this," Mrs Kline says. She still seems shocked to see her husband after several months.

"Is there a garden shed I can sleep in?" Mr Kline asks.

"Normally, I wouldn't even put the dog in a

place like that, but as its just for a few hours and we don't know anything about you, maybe it's okay." Mrs Sense goes off to grab some bedding for him. She is glad it's not so cold outside at this time of year.

"Well, I've been sleeping in fields. So, this will be like a hotel!" Patrick says to no one in particular.

"Oh dear, why has all this happened to us?" Mrs Kline asks.

"Let's talk about that in the morning." Mrs Sense has returned. Mr Sense shows Mr Kline to the garden shed and then they all go back to sleep.

The next day, they gather for a family meeting. Mr Kline explains how he lost his job after making some bad choices at work. He lost all the money in his business and ended up being sent to prison for fraud. Joseph is shocked to hear this as he had believed his father had left them. He isn't sure which option is worse....

"How can we help you to get back on your feet?" Mr Sense has taken the day off work and is thinking practically. "I guess you will need an address whilst you sort out a house to move to?"

"Yes, that's always the problem. They want a fixed address but I can't get one unless I have money. It's like an impossible situation," Mr

Kline feels desperate.

"Nothing is impossible with God." Mrs Sense drops a Bible verse into the conversation. "You can use our address. In fact, one of us will go with you to the government office today to see if we can get you emergency housing."

"Oh, you don't need to trouble yourselves. You've been enough help already." Mrs Kline is embarrassed by their situation.

"We want to help you. I'm sure you would do the same if you found someone in need," Mrs Sense says. The Kline's look at each other. They're not sure whether they would be *as* helpful especially to someone that had broken into their house!

"Now that we've got your story straight and know that you aren't a burglar, you can move into our house with your family until you can get a proper place to live. God has blessed us with a lot of space," Mr Sense offers.

Mrs Kline looks hopeful. They all sit down to have breakfast. Reuben and Joseph discuss Reuben's books. Reuben finds that he enjoys sharing his adventures with Joseph. In fact, it's more fun than having them on his own. Ellie and Jessica talk about fairies and princesses.

After breakfast, Mr Sense takes Mr Kline to enquire about housing in the area. When they arrive back, Mr and Mrs Kline go for a long walk to talk about things whilst the Sense adults supervise all of the children.

The government agree to provide housing in the area but it will take a few weeks to organise. The Kline's are grateful for the Sense family's offer. They plan to stay with them for a few weeks.

Mr Kline makes friends with Dodgy after getting an injection at the hospital. The window is repaired.

The Kline's go to church with the Sense's on Sundays and Patrick is especially interested in the teaching. "You know, I heard all this stuff years ago in Sunday school but I just thought it was a load of stories. It didn't occur to me that it might be true. Now, I've seen what happens when I go my own way and give in to greed. I nearly lost my family. I'm not going to let that happen again. I need God to help me." Mr Kline says all this to Mr Sense after they have been to church one day.

"God already paid the price for the things we do wrong when he sent His Son Jesus to die for us. All you need to do is to believe that and to turn away from those things that are wrong. Then live a new life following Jesus." Mr Sense hopes his words will be helpful to his new friend. He feels sorry for the man and knows that he could have been in the same situation if he had made different choices in his life.

The Kline family move into their new house after just a few weeks and Patrick manages to find a job in the area. He later becomes a Christian and continues taking his family along to church. Reuben is thrilled that Joseph is in his Sunday School class and they go on to become good friends reading stories together and having many adventures.

Go to 111.

42.

Reuben rushes up to his room and begins sorting through his things. He is making such a noise that his mum appears in his doorway.

"Reuben, what on earth are you doing?" Mrs Sense asks him.

"There is a new boy at school. He is dirty and poor and he doesn't have any uniform. I thought I would give him some of my things," Reuben explains. He expects his mum to praise him.

"Reuben, wait, come and sit down." Mrs Sense needs to think how she should deal with this. She doesn't want to stop Reuben being generous but she knows that giving away his old toys, that he doesn't want anymore, could be taken in the wrong way.

"Why, Mum? The Bible says that we should share what we have with the poor. That's what Jesus did...isn't it?" Reuben continues sorting and the pile of old junk gets bigger and bigger.

"Yes, Reuben, but wait. We need to pray about this and I need to think about how we can properly help this family in the right way." Mrs Sense pulls him over to sit down.

"What's his name?" she asks.

"Joseph, he just started at school today," Reuben answers. He has given up fighting his mum. He knows she is usually right about things and he doesn't really want to give away so many of his toys anyway! He decides to listen.

"I think I will phone your school and find out what the teachers know about this boy, if he's just started," Mrs Sense decides.

42Q. What will Reuben say?

A. No, don't do that mum, I don't want to talk to him again anyway. Go to 62.

B. Yes, that's a good idea, Go to 63.

43.

Reuben watches Joseph standing outside for a few seconds. "Mum," he yells.

Mrs Sense comes down the stairs. She looks alarmed. "Reuben, why are you shouting? Noah is asleep!" she whispers to him.

"Look out of this window." Reuben points to where Joseph had been standing but he has already gone.

Go back to 17Q and decide what Reuben will do instead.

44.

Reuben forgets about Joseph as he rushes off to plan his ninth birthday party. He needs to decide who he will invite and what he wants to do. He sits down and begins making a list of his classmates starting with his closest friends....

He had planned to invite everyone in his class as well as some people he knows from other schools. He suddenly realises that he needs to decide whether he will invite Joseph...

44Q. What will Reuben decide?

A. No, Joseph is new and can't expect to be invited. Go to 73.

B. Yes, It will be good for Joseph to make new friends. <u>*Go to 56.*</u>

C. Only those who can bring a present worth more than £10 and some food to share are allowed to come. <u>*Go to 74.*</u>

45.

Camping has always been a special event for Reuben. His parents have allowed him to do it a few times in the garden of their house.

"I'd love to be able to camp all of the time, it must be so exciting, you are so lucky," Reuben says to Joseph.

Joseph looks shocked and ashamed, "We didn't choose to be in this position. Living in a small tent with three of us is not so much fun when it might be for a very long time."

"Where is your dad?" Reuben asks.

"I don't have a dad anymore," Joseph says.

"Everyone has a dad." Reuben doesn't understand what Joseph means.

"I mean, I did have a dad, but he left us before we came here. He lost all of our money," Joseph explains.

"Oh, Reuben, I don't think you will ever understand this. You have a mum and dad and a nice house and lots of things, I bet," Joseph guesses.

"Yes, that's true. I think my mum would know what to do to help you," Reuben says.

"We don't need your help, we're fine here. Hopefully, we will get some money from the government soon, enough to rent a small flat. I'm also going to start doing some jobs for local people," Joseph tells him.

"Wouldn't it be easier if people just gave you money and some things?" Reuben doesn't understand why Joseph won't accept help. In his mind it's simple: Joseph's family needs help, Reuben's family can help them.

45Q. *What will Reuben say now?*

A. "I'm sure my church will help you if we ask them." <u>Go to 46.</u>

B. "Do you mind if I tell my parents that you are here?" <u>Go to 47.</u>

C. "I'll help you find some jobs in the village as I know people here." <u>Go to 75.</u>

46.

Reuben blurts out the first thing that comes into his head. "I'm sure my church will help you if we ask them."

Joseph looks ashamed. "No, we don't need help and definitely not from religious people. We aren't beggars. We will get a flat in town soon. I'm going to get some jobs in the village to help my mum pay for our food. The government will also help us soon."

"Okay, can I help you get some jobs here then because I know some people who need things doing?" Reuben wants to help and realises that he needs to allow Joseph to make the decisions.

"Yes, I think that would be the best thing you could do, but please don't tell your parents, Reuben," Joseph adds.

Go to 75.

47.

Reuben knows he needs an adult to help. "Do you mind if I tell my parents you're here?" he asks carefully.

Joseph considers his request for a second or two. "I think that would be okay but only if they won't tell everyone else. I'm not even sure if the school would allow me to attend if they knew we were living in a tent! It won't be for long though." Joseph doesn't sound sure about the last part.

"Would you like to come back to my house,?

You can meet my parents for yourself. I've already met your mum," Reuben says. He realises it might have been better for him to have met Joseph's mum when he wasn't spying on her through some trees!

"Yes, that sounds good. I should tell my mum first as she will be worried about what's going to happen now that you've found us. I'll tell her everything will be okay." Joseph appears to have control of the situation. He's making decisions that Reuben wouldn't know how to make. Reuben is grateful that he has a mum and dad and a house!

The two boys walk round to the tent area and Joseph introduces his mum and little sister to Reuben. Reuben greets them shyly. Joseph's mum offers him an apple but he decides they probably need it more than he does.

"No, please take it," Joseph says. "We have an apple tree behind here and no one seems to be eating any of the fruit. It just falls to the ground and rots."

"Can I quickly look inside your tent? Reuben asks. He wants to know what it would be like to fit all of his things inside such a small space with three people as well.

"Sure, well now that you've found our spot, you may as well see everything," Joseph laughs. "Let me show you around." He crawls into the small entrance and Reuben follows.

"Wow, it's really very small." Reuben is shocked by the lack of space and the few things that are in the tent.

"We had to sell a lot of our things," Joseph says. "As you can see, there is barely room for us let alone lots of stuff, but at least we don't have to worry about things being stolen." He tries to make a joke. Reuben doesn't laugh. He can't imagine what it would be like to live here all of the time and not to have any things at all. It must be so boring. What about when it's really cold or really hot, or rainy or even snowy!? He must find a way to help the family but he knows he will need to do it without upsetting them.

"Right, let's go to my house," Reuben says. He knows that Joseph will be shocked by the size of his house and all of his things but it's too late to worry about that now.

The two boys set off after Joseph's mum gives permission for Joseph to go to Reuben's house for a bit. They arrive at Reuben's about thirty minutes later than Mrs Sense had been expecting Reuben home.

"Reuben, where have you been? I was worried about you. Oh, sorry, who is this?" Mrs Sense sees Joseph and turns to Reuben.

"I'm Joseph, a friend of Reuben's from school. It's nice to meet you, Ma'am." Joseph puts on his most polite voice and shakes hands.

"Well come in Joseph, we've enough food for one extra tonight. Would you like to stay for dinner? Does your mum know where you are?" Mrs Sense asks.

"Yes, she does, I just met her in the field by their tent," Reuben says. He doesn't really know how to start the conversation about Joseph's living situation so he decides that just telling the truth is best.

Joseph looks a little embarrassed but nods to confirm. "We're only living there for a little while because my dad left after he lost all of our money." Joseph decides to tell the kind lady who's just offered him dinner everything. He explains how they came to be in the tent and how he is worried about his mum trying to provide for them.

"Oh, Joseph, I'm so sorry to hear that. It's really good that you met Reuben so that we could talk about this. I think the first thing to do is to pray. What do you think Reuben?" Mrs Sense turns to Reuben and waits for his response.

47Q. What will Reuben say?

A. *"Mum, you are so embarrassing."* <u>Go to 76.</u>

B. *"No, we need to do something to help!*

now" *Go to 77.*

C. *"Yes, let's pray first."* *Go to 78.*

48.

"Mum, Mum," Reuben yells. "There's a boy outside staring at our house!"

Mrs Sense comes running in from the garden. "Oh, there you are Reuben, you were later than I was expecting. What has happened to your knee? Oh, and it's still bleeding. Let's get it bandaged up quickly." Mrs Sense focuses on the obvious problem although Reuben is distracted. She is used to the various injuries that boys seem to end up with.

"But, there's a boy outside. He walked home with me. Can we invite him in?" Reuben asks.

"What? Where?" Mrs Sense is confused. "So, you know this boy?" She walks to the window and looks out. There is no-one there.

"Yes, his name is Joseph, he started in my class today. I think his family might be poor," Reuben adds.

"Well, where is he?" Mrs Sense is still looking out of the window.

Reuben's knee now has a large bandage covering the cut. He looks out of the window but Joseph has definitely gone.

Maybe Reuben should've invited Joseph to come in straight away rather than leaving him standing in the street! Now that he has gone, Reuben will have to focus on something else.

Go to 44.

49.

Reuben has put two and two together and suspects that Joseph is connected with the people in the tent. "So your mum calls you Joe?" he asks.

Joseph goes a little red. "I guess I'll just leave you in the ditch if you don't want my help. Good luck getting home." Joseph starts to walk away.

Reuben calls after him, "Wait, WAIT!"

Joseph has already disappeared. Reuben is left bleeding in the ditch. He wishes he had just asked for Joseph's help instead of trying to be a detective and figure everything out. Joseph obviously didn't want to tell him about his connection with the people in the tent or he wouldn't have pretended not to know them. If only Reuben had waited until a bit later to ask his questions of Joseph, he might have been out of the ditch and on his way home by now.

Reuben lies there and waits. He shouts for

help a few times but no one hears him. He is all alone and starting to get cold. He shivers. He prays that someone will find him soon before it gets dark.

"Reuben, Reuben," He hears the voice of his dad and bursts into sobs.

"I'm here, Dad. Please get me out of here!" he half yells and half cries.

"What happened? Reuben, where are you?" Mr Sense reaches the edge of the ditch and leans over the edge.

"Oh, what happened to your knee? How long have you been there and how did you get there in the first place? You must be very cold." Mr Sense keeps talking as he reaches down and picks Reuben up. He carries him in his strong arms.

As they get near to the pink tent, Reuben suddenly remembers how he got into the mess in the first place. "Wait, dad, look over there," he says excitedly.

"What, what is it?" Mr Sense asks. He can't see anything.

"There were people living in a pink tent here. One of them came to my school today. I was watching them but they saw me and chased me, that's how I fell in the ditch," Reuben explains.

"What, did they see you fall in the ditch? Who are these people? Why didn't they help you get out?" Mr Sense is angry now.

"I think it's my fault Dad. The boy, Joseph, offered to help me but I asked him a question about his family that he didn't like, so he left." Reuben feels guilty again.

"Well, where are they now?" Mr Sense looks around.

There is no sign of the tent or the people but it's obvious that people have been staying in the area. There are a few pieces of rubbish lying around and a black patch on the ground where the people had been cooking.

"I guess they really didn't want to be found. Do you know why they were living in their tent?" Mr Sense is worried about the people.

"No, I didn't really pay enough attention to Joseph at school," Reuben admits.

The family have gone. Joseph doesn't return to Reuben's school. They might still be in the area but Reuben doesn't meet them again. He has missed his opportunity to get to know Joseph and to be his friend. That's a bit of a shame. If he wants to try again he will need to start the story again and make different choices. Go to 1.

50.

Let's think about this. Joseph is offering to

help. There is no one else around. Reuben is stuck in a ditch with an injury. How is he going to sort himself out? <u>Go back to 21Q</u> and think again!

51.

Reuben decides that the whole thing has gone too far already and he wishes that he hadn't got involved. He should've just ignored the tent in the field and carried on his way. He is tired and there is a book he wants to read before he goes to sleep.

Mr Jack doesn't seem to have any ideas either so Reuben gives up. "Let's go home now, Mr Jack. I think we've done all we can," he says.

"Well, actually, you haven't really done anything apart from talking to me," Mrs Kline points out. "That's okay though as there isn't really anything that can be done. We just need to wait for the government to sort things out. I hope Joe manages to get some work as well, then we can at least have money for food."

Mr Jack decides that he is doing enough by allowing the family to stay on his land without reporting them to the police. "Make sure you don't burn my grass or leave your rubbish lying around when you leave," he says. He wags his finger at them.

"Come on Ellie, let's go," Reuben calls. Ellie doesn't want to leave but as Reuben is meant to be the leader of this trip, she climbs out of the tent and follows him. Mr Jack, Reuben and Ellie walk back to the Sense's house.

Mr Sense is home from work and Mrs Sense has been waiting for an update. She has told him about the tent and how Reuben and Ellie have gone to investigate with the big farmer.

She opens the door as soon as she sees them arriving, "Well?" she asks.

"Well, what?" Reuben says. "There's a mum living in the tent with a boy from my class and his little sister."

"I told them not to burn my grass or to leave rubbish around. I think that's quite fair." Mr Jack says.

"But, but…," Mrs Sense can't quite believe that Mr Jack has just left the family in the woods in a tent! "How will they manage? Can't we help them in some way?"

"I didn't really know what to do and Reuben here was keen to get back to his reading." Mr Jack explains.

"Oh." Mr and Mrs Sense say together.

It looks like the story has come to a sudden end because Reuben would rather read an adventure than have an adventure in real life. He has also forgotten that the Bible tells us to help those in need. There were a lot of things he could have done to try and help the family but he was more interested in his own comfort and doing his own things. Mr Jack must just have been having a bad day.

However, Reuben is the decision maker and he has decided not to do anything about this family in the tent. If he changes his mind and decides that something does need to be done, he will have to start the story again and make different decisions. <u>Go to 1.</u>

52.

Reuben feels sure that his parents would want to help this family. He forgets that he is just eight years old and that he cannot possibly make that type of decision by himself.

"You should all come home with me." He announces.

Ellie pops her head out of the tent, "Yes, come and live at our house. That would be so much fun. I would have a new best friend and we could play all of the time."

Mr Jack looks alarmed "No, Reuben, Ellie. I don't think when your mum said you could come with me to check things out that she would have been expecting you to bring home a family of people!"

"But, the Bible does tell us to help poor people, doesn't it, Mr Jack?" Reuben can't see what the problem is. To his mind, it's a simple case of doing what the Bible says.

"Yes, it definitely says that we should help, Reuben, but we need to work out the best way to help," Mr Jack explains.

Mrs Kline has been listening to their conversation, "The Bible? Oh, are you religious then?" she asks sounding disappointed.

"My wife and I are Christians, yes. We go to a church on the other side of the village just down the road from our farm. Reuben and Ellie's family are also Christians but they attend a church a little way out of the village," Mr Jack tells her.

"We don't need your charity. We can help ourselves." Mrs Kline suddenly seems cold towards them. "I guess that means you won't get your reward from God for helping us." She looks away from Mr Jack. "I thought you were all just being kind."

"We do really want to help you," Mr Jack says. "Not because of any reward from God, but because we care about you and want to obey the Bible."

Reuben has been trying to work things out while they are talking. He blurts out, "Can they go and live with you at your farm then Mr Jack. You have lots of space."

Go to 79.

53.

Reuben has a crazy moment. He forgets his injured knee and rushes back outside. He runs down his garden path. He shouts at the top of his lungs "MY HOUSE IS BIGGER THAN YOURS, HAHA!"

There is no response. He looks around for Joseph but he has already gone. Maybe he had already gone when Reuben made his mad dash outside. Either way, Reuben looks very silly.

A few of Reuben's neighbours appear at their windows and one man walks down his garden path to see who is yelling in the street.

Mrs Sense comes running out of their house. She grabs Reuben's arms and drags him back inside. "What is wrong with you, Reuben. There's no one there. Have you gone mad??"

Let's go back to 24Q and think again, shall we?

54.

Reuben opens the door and smiles at Mr Jack. "Right, let's go," he says.

"Okay, Reuben. But is there someone crying?" Mr Jack looks around and over the top of Reuben's head.

"Yes," Mrs Sense answers. "I'm afraid that's Ellie, She wanted to go with the two of you but Reuben said that she couldn't."

"Oh, that's a shame, Reuben. I'm sure we could take your little sister as well. I'll make sure you get to lead any adventures that we have!" Mr Jack offers.

"I guess Ellie can come." Reuben realises that he doesn't really have a choice. He also wants to please the big farmer who is being kind by agreeing to take him in the first place.

Mrs Sense acts quickly, "Ellie, come here, please. Right, you will need your boots and coat."

Ellie comes running, her tears have suddenly dried.

"Reuben, I want you to think about your attitude towards your sister for next time please." Mrs Sense is still disappointed but she knows that now isn't the time to get into it.

Go to 55

55.

Ellie is ready for an adventure. She grabs her boots and coat and stands behind Reuben.

"Let's go then, kids. I'll have them back within the hour," Mr Jack addresses Mrs Sense.

"Thankyou Mr Jack, no hurry," Mrs Sense is relaxed and curious!

Mr Jack leads Reuben and Ellie down the path and back towards Reuben's school. "Right, you lead the way, Reuben, as you were the one who saw the tent."

Reuben steps forward proudly and heads back to where he saw the tent. They walk through a wooded area and at last come to the edge of the field. The pink tent stands out in the greenery. There is still no-one around and the tent is zipped up.

Mr Jack says, "This might be the other half of a mystery that I've been trying to solve for a while."

Reuben doesn't know what he is talking about. "What do you mean?" he asks.

"I can't say anything yet, but I think I might know who is living here." The farmer obviously knows something that Reuben doesn't and Ellie is too young to really understand. "Let's have a look around."

They approach the tent cautiously. "Hello, is

anyone here? Hello, hello."

The tent starts to open and a woman looks out. She has probably been sleeping and her eyes look red. "Hi, is everything okay?" she asks.

"I think I should be asking you that question. What are you doing here? I own this land," Mr Jack tells her.

"Oh, I'm so sorry. We'll only be staying for a few days," the lady answers quickly.

"No, I'm not worried about you camping on my land. That's fine. I'm concerned about why you are living in a tent. Is it just you?" Mr Jack tries to speak softly so as not to scare the lady.

"Look, look," Reuben calls. He is holding up some clothing hanging on a rope that is being used as a washing line. The rope has been tied to two trees. "This uniform is from my school!"

"Yes, that's Joseph's. He started there today. He must be about your age," the lady says to Reuben.

"Yes, I saw him." Reuben feels very guilty that he hadn't made more effort with Joseph.

"A teacher gave him some old uniform but it had been in a cupboard for a long time and smelled quite dusty so I washed it in the stream." The lady points to a small trickle of water running nearby.

Mr Jack is amazed that there is a child living in the tent. It doesn't look big enough for two people. A little head then pops up next to the lady, "Who is it, Mum?"

"Oh! "Mr Jack jumps back and Reuben and Ellie stare at the little girl. She must be a little younger than Ellie.

"What's your name?" Ellie says.

"Jessica and I'm four," the girl responds.

"I'm Ellie and I'm six, That's my brother Reuben, he's eight," Ellie tells her.

The lady smiles, "Well, at least the children are getting on well."

"Why are you here though? If Joseph has enrolled in the local school, you're not just on a camping holiday are you?" Mr Jack asks.

The lady looks as if she might cry. "My husband left after he lost all of our money. We don't have anywhere else to go. We're waiting for the government to help us, but I don't know if they will."

Reuben is shocked. He hadn't thought that people could end up in this situation. He has always had a house and a lot of things.

Mr Jack looks thoughtful. "Your husband left?" he asks.

"Yes." The lady doesn't want to give any further details and Mr Jack decides to leave things as they are for now.

"Can I ask for your name?" Mr Jack suddenly realises that he hasn't even got basic details from the lady.

"I'm Elaine Kline. Joseph is eight and Jessica, four. I didn't send Jessica to pre-school as she didn't have any proper clothes at all," Mrs Kline explains.

Reuben thinks to himself that he wouldn't have described the rags that Joseph was wearing as clothes, but he says nothing. He is still in shock.

"Yes, so, where is Joseph?" Mr Jack asks.

"He might be in the village looking for some work. I think he was going to try and find some odd jobs to buy us some food," Mrs Kline says.

"Joseph has to work?" Reuben can hardly believe what he is hearing. He is the same age as Joseph and never has to think about things like this. He feels very grateful for his own family.

Ellie has climbed inside the tent and she and Jessica are playing happily. Reuben is glad that Ellie came with them. She seems to have made a friend.

Mr Jack looks thoughtful. He doesn't really know what to do about the situation. Reuben has some ideas though.

55Q. *What will Reuben say?*

A. "Mr Jack, the Bible says that we should help those who are in need. I want to take them home to my house." *Go to 52.*

B. *"Mr Jack, I think we should go home now. There's nothing we can really do."* <u>Go to 51.</u>

C. *"Mr Jack, you have a big farm with lots of space, don't you? Why don't you take them home?* <u>Go to 79.</u>

D. *"Mr Jack, I think we should ask the police to deal with this. Maybe they will be able to get the government to give them a house!"* <u>Go to 80.</u>

56.

Reuben spends quite a bit of time writing a list of everyone in his class. Then he writes the invitations to his party. He gathers all of his invitations together and puts them in his school bag.

"How many children are you inviting to your party, Reuben?" Mrs Sense asks.

"Everyone in my class," Reuben says.

"Right, I need to make sure we have a few extra adults around to supervise the bouncy castle," Mrs Sense tells him.

The next day, Reuben heads to school as usual. He is excited about giving out his invitations. He has spent quite a bit of time making them look professional. He knows that most of the children in his class will look forward to his party. He feels pleased that some of the poorer children will get the chance to have a great afternoon.

Mrs Gibbs is teaching as Mr Gately has a day off. She allows Reuben to make an announcement to the class about his party.

He stands at the front of the class. "I'm having a birthday party on Saturday and you are all invited!" he says.

Reuben goes around the classroom handing out the invitations. "You can also come if you like, Mrs Gibbs." he offers. The children laugh. Mrs Gibbs probably has better things to do than attending every child's party every year!

Go to 85.

57.

Reuben is frustrated and decides that he has already done enough to befriend Joseph. He doesn't speak to him again even though he sees him around at school and in class. Some of Reuben's friends seem to become friendly with Joseph but Reuben doesn't bother. He focuses on his own life and forgets about Joseph completely.

Well, that's a pretty boring end to what could have been an interesting story. It sounds like

Reuben needs to learn that friendships can be hard work. He also needs to learn not to give up so easily. He has missed an opportunity to be a good friend to Joseph. Maybe he should try reading the story again and make different decisions next time. Go to 1.

58.

Reuben decides that he needs to investigate. Joseph is just so strange!

After school the next day, he quickly gets up and follows Joseph as he leaves the classroom. He doesn't speak to him as he knows that Joseph probably won't want to talk to him.

Go to 35.

59.

Reuben knows he has gotten himself into a muddle by trying to be helpful but upsetting Joseph in the process. He prays that God will help him know what to do. After praying he feels that saying sorry probably won't be enough. His birthday is coming up and he is having a big party. He decides to invite Joseph to show him that he cares.

Go to 56.

60.

Reuben knows that it's not really polite to invite himself to someone else's house. But he is so curious about Joseph that he can't help himself.

Joseph looks shocked when Reuben invites himself but he nods to show that Reuben can come. Reuben checks with his mum who agrees. She is pleased that Reuben is befriending Joseph. The two boys set off across the village together. Joseph is quite quiet but Reuben chats away about anything he can think of.

They walk for a long time. Joseph keeps looking at the houses as they walk past. They reach one at the corner of a street that seems to be separate from the others in the area. Joseph stops near the drive.

"Is this your house then?" Reuben asks.

"Yeah," Joseph says but he doesn't sound very confident. He starts to walk up the driveway. There are no cars around and nothing to suggest anyone is home. "I don't think my mum is home from work yet. Maybe you should visit another time," he says.

"Okay, but how are you going to get in?"

Reuben asks. There's something not quite right about this situation. Reuben also thinks that he remembers visiting the people that live in this house with his family when they first moved to the village. Joseph's family definitely hadn't been there. The house belonged to an older couple. Maybe Joseph's grandparents live here?

"There's a key hidden somewhere outside but I'm not allowed to tell anyone where it is," Joseph says.

"Oh, okay." This makes sense to Reuben and he turns to leave. "I hope I can come another time then."

"Yes, that would be good," Joseph responds.

60Q. What will Reuben do?

A. Ask again if he can go inside. <u>Go to 86.</u>
B. Leave and go home. <u>Go to 87.</u>
C. Spy on Joseph. <u>Go to 88.</u>

61.

The next day at school Joseph comes straight over to Reuben. "I've finished the first book. It was great. I'm going to read the next one later. Can you bring the third one in the series to school tomorrow and maybe the fourth as well?"

He hands a book back to Reuben. Reuben looks at it.

"Oh, sorry about that. My little sister got hold of it for a while. I tried to clean it up as best I could."Joseph grins and looks a bit awkward. "It's a really great story though, I loved it. I felt like I was really having the adventure myself and it made life seem easier for a while."

Reuben swallows. The book is very dirty and looks as if something has tried to eat it! This is exactly what he had thought might happen.

61Q. How will he respond?

A. Suggest Joseph uses the public library. *Go to 89.*

B. Cry about the damage to one of his favourite books. *Go to 90.*

C. Accept what has happened and agree to lend more books to Joseph. *Go to 91.*

62.

Reuben doesn't want to create such a big fuss about nothing. He knows that if his mum phones the school and gets more information, then he will be forced to get very involved with Joseph. Reuben had thought that he could just do his bit and then return to his other friends. He likes his life as it is and doesn't want things to change.

"Don't phone the school Mum. Let's just leave it," Reuben says.

Mrs Sense looks confused. "Reuben, you seemed very concerned about Joseph a few minutes ago. You can't just tell me about something like this and expect me not to do something about it. You seemed to want to help. What would Jesus do, do you think?"

It looks like Mrs Sense is going to phone the school anyway whether Reuben likes it or not!

Go to 63.

63.

"Hello, Mrs Gibbs? Yes, this is Reuben's mum." Mrs Sense pauses and then speaks again, "Reuben has come home talking about a poor boy Joseph that started at his school today. He said he doesn't even have uniform and that he is really dirty!?"

"I'm sorry Mrs Sense, he just turned up this morning. His mother did bring him but she left again before we really had a chance to speak to her properly. She just said that the family were going through some sort of financial problem,"

Mrs Gibbs explains. She knows she needs to be careful about giving out too much information but she knows that Mrs Sense isn't a gossip and might actually be able to help Joseph's family.

"Do you know where they live? I guess they must be on the edge of the village in the cheap flats?" Mrs Sense tries to say this without sounding too posh. She knows that her family has been blessed by God in a lot of ways.

"To be honest, Joseph was really very dirty. I wondered if they might even be living on the street or something like that," Mrs Gibbs admits.

"WHAT?! In our village?!" Mrs Sense can't believe this is even possible.

Mrs Gibbs wishes now that she had done more to find out about Joseph's situation. It shouldn't have taken a phone call from a parent to wake her up. "I guess I should call the social services people to try and find the family."

"No, don't do that yet. There are plenty of families from the church who would help if they were needed. I think we just need to be careful about how we offer them help. We don't want them to think they are in any trouble," Mrs Sense finishes.

"Okay, yes, it's a difficult one. I think I'll try and talk to Joseph at school tomorrow and find out what's really going on. I'll let you know if there's anything you can do. Thank you for calling Mrs Sense." Mrs Gibbs hangs up the phone.

Mrs Gibbs thinks about things for a little while and then picks up the phone to report the matter to social services. She is worried that she should have done this earlier and that she might be blamed if something were to happen to the family.

The social services department, in turn, contacts the police. It is their duty to report any cases where children might not be being looked after properly.

Neither department can find any record of the Kline family having moved into the area from the details given. There is a record from Sunnywild, a town not that far away. A mother and two children with the surname Kline had to leave their house when the father was sent to prison. He was convicted of stealing money from a business. It had happened just three months ago. Patrick Kline, the father, was released from prison a month ago but his current whereabouts are not known.

The police decide to search the area to see if they can find Patrick or any members of his family. After searching for a while, they find an area fairly near to the school where someone has been camping recently. There is a bit of rubbish left and some black grass where someone has been cooking. The people have obviously gone now though. The police close their file and report their findings to the social services who also close theirs. They phone the school and advise Mrs Gibbs of the result of their search. She decides to speak to Joseph at school as originally planned.

Joseph doesn't come back to school and is not seen again in the area. The family must've moved on.

This appears to be a dead end. Let's see what would have happened if Reuben had followed Joseph to his house at an earlier stage. <u>Go to 35.</u>

64.

Reuben isn't really thinking and he just loves climbing trees. He gets distracted from his goal of following Joseph and instead climbs a very tall tree a little further into the woodland. The trees are very close together here and he can't see much, apart from leaves and branches all around. He settles down into part of the trunk and gets an Enid Blyton book out of his bag. It is called *The Wishing Chair*. Reuben wishes he could fly as he reads the story about the chair with wings. He forgets what he was meant to be doing and loses track of the time. It starts to get dark and he pulls out a torch to continue reading one of his favourite stories. He falls asleep and his book crashes to the ground. A fairy and a pixie find him as they are returning to Fairyland. The fairy sprays him with magic dust and they float all the way home to Reuben's house…….

Wait, this is a real story about real things that happened to a boy named Reuben Sense. There are plenty of pixie and fairy stories around if you want to read those. Reuben did not climb another tree as he realised it would be a waste of time. He followed Joseph through the forest instead! <u>Go to 35.</u>

65.

What?! Joseph is now inviting Reuben to follow him. Why would he decide to go home at this point? He might be about to solve the mystery or at least make some progress!

However, it is Reuben who has to make these decisions not me. I'm just a humble story teller and shouldn't really have an opinion.

65Q. What will Reuben do?
A. Go home. <u>Go to 92.</u>

B. Go with Joseph. Go to 66.

66.

They walk further into the woods until they come to the edge of a field. A pink tent is sitting there. It is zipped up.

Reuben is confused. "You are camping here?" he asks.

"No, we live here but just until we can get a new house," Joseph explains. "My mum and sister are probably asleep in the tent now. They weren't feeling well earlier. We think it might be the water from the stream."

Reuben is silent. Of all the things that he had considered, this hadn't been one of them. Joseph's family live in a tent! He decides to focus on the positive side.

Go to 45.

67.

It's been a hard day for Reuben as he's watched his friends enjoying spending time with other people and he has been all alone. He knows it's his own fault but it's still been difficult. He knows that Todd is offering him a chance to be included again.

"Yes, I would like to come. Do you think your mum will be able to call mine when we get to your house?" Reuben asks. He tries to pretend that everything is okay.

"Yes, I'll ask her. I'm sure it will be fine. Daniel was telling me how much he likes reading. I know you have a lot of books as you've lent me some of your Enid Blyton books before. Would Daniel be able to borrow one or two, do you think?" Todd asks him.

67Q. What will Reuben say?

A. No, I don't lend my books. <u>Go to 93.</u>
B. Yes, of course, he can. <u>Go to 94.</u>

68.

As soon as the words are out of his mouth Reuben wishes he could take them back.

Todd looks like he might explode with anger. "Reuben, Mr Gately told me that you tried to push Daniel and Joseph together because they are both poor kids. What is wrong with you? We are all the same. I don't think I want to be friends with someone who behaves like this, I really don't. If you want to force me to choose between you and Daniel, then I choose Daniel. It didn't have to be like this as I thought we could all be friends together but it's your decision. Let's go, Daniel," Todd finishes.

Reuben watches them walk away and suddenly has a change of heart. "I'm sorry Todd, Daniel. You're right. I shouldn't have said that. I really am sorry. I would like to join you."

Todd softens and looks at him, "Okay, Reuben, I know you aren't normally like this. Let's forget about it and go and have a good time, okay?"

Go to 67.

69.

Reuben doesn't want to admit that he misses his friends and feels lonely. He decides he would rather go home by himself and sulk in his bedroom.

He walks home feeling sorry for himself. He quietly opens the door of his house.

"Reuben, is that you?" Mrs Sense calls, "How was your day at school?"

"Fine. I just want to go to bed Mum." He starts walking upstairs.

"So, you don't want any dinner then?" Mrs Sense knows that if Reuben refuses food then something is really wrong!

"No, I'm not hungry," Reuben answers as he shuts his bedroom door.

Mrs Sense decides to give him a while to think. Something has obviously happened at school and he isn't yet ready to talk about it.

A bit later she goes up to his room and knocks on the door.

"Who is it?" Reuben says although he knows it will be his mum.

"Me," she answers. "Can I come in?"

"I suppose so," Reuben says.

Mrs Sense walks in and sits on the floor. "What happened at school today then Reuben?" she asks.

Reuben is ready to talk. "Well, it started when a new boy came to our class. Mr Gately asked me to look after him because I'm a Christian. I thought it would be too difficult as Joseph's different to me and I already have friends. I asked if Daniel could be his friend instead. But then, Mr Gately must've asked Jack to be friends with Joseph and Todd to be friends with Daniel so I was left all on my own." Reuben starts to cry. "They were all sitting together but I was sitting on my own."

Mrs Sense puts her arm around him and tries to make sense of his story. "Okay, so why didn't you want to be friends with Joseph?"

"Because he is dirty and his clothes are torn. I thought my other friends might make fun of me and I really don't need any more friends, Mum. I have Jack and Todd," Reuben says through his tears. "But, now I don't have Jack and Todd," he starts sobbing.

"Reuben, can't you all be friends together? It sounds as if Jack and Todd are quite happy to be friends with Joseph and Daniel. I'm sure they would include you." Mrs Sense is thinking logically.

"I don't want everything to change though. I like my friends." Reuben is starting to calm down a little.

"What would Jesus want you to do, though, Reuben? Do you think He would reject someone just because they are different to Him?" Mrs Sense says this gently as she knows it will be difficult for him to hear.

"Well, Todd did still ask me to go to his house with Daniel as well, but I said 'no' and came home instead." Reuben realises that Todd was already trying to include him.

"There you are, see." Mrs Sense tries to be patient with Reuben as she knows that these friendships are important to him. "Why don't you invite all of them to your party that's coming up, then they will see that you want to be their friend?"

"I could do that I suppose, I don't think Joseph or Daniel probably has enough money to bring me a gift though." Reuben is thinking out loud.

"Reuben, that's really not what you should be thinking about, is it?" Mrs Sense tries to keep his mind on being kind and caring for other people rather than how he can use them!

"No, okay Mum, I will write the invitations now."

Go to 56.

70.

Reuben can see that Joseph is hiding something. "What's in your hands?" he asks.

"Nothing, what do you mean?" Joseph answers. He looks down and won't look at Reuben's face.

Reuben moves towards him. "I think you are holding something behind your back. What is it?" he asks.

Joseph says nothing as Reuben gets closer.

"Come on, please, just show me. I won't tell anyone," Reuben says.

Joseph looks at Reuben and sees that he means it. Maybe he can trust him. "It's just this, I was hungry." He holds out half a sandwich.

Reuben realises that it must be the remains of Mr Gately's lunch. "Where did you get it? Mr Gately will be really mad if you went in his desk." Reuben looks scared.

"It was in the bin, just there." Joseph points to a small bin underneath the desk. "I saw him throw it in there earlier and I was just so hungry," he adds.

"Why don't you have any food? You really need to tell someone if you are so hungry," Reuben says.

"My family are just having some problems at the moment. We don't have much money for things but we'll be okay." Joseph looks sad and a bit worried. "You won't tell anyone, will you?"

"No, I won't say anything for now. Here, you can have the rest of my lunch as well." Reuben hands him a few bits and pieces and watches Joseph's face light up as he takes them.

"When do you think you will have money again?" Reuben asks.

"I don't know but we should get a house soon...." Joseph says without thinking.

"You don't even have a house!?" Reuben is shocked. "Where do you live then?"

"In a tent at the edge of a field," Joseph says.

"Just one tent, how do you fit?" Reuben can't imagine it. He has his own room and lives in a big house with lots of things.

"It's just me, mum and my little sister," Joseph explains.

At this point, their conversation is disturbed by Mr Gately coming back into the classroom. Mr Gately jumps when he sees the boys as he had thought everyone had left for the day.

"What are you doing here boys?" he asks.

70Q. What will Reuben say?

A. "Joseph was hungry and looking for food." Go to 96.

B. "Nothing, we were just talking." Go to 97.

71.

Reuben decides to ignore the fact that Joseph is trying to hide something and to focus on being his friend.

"Shall we go home?" he says.

Joseph nods and as Reuben turns his back to leave the classroom he hears a noise as Joseph drops something into the bin under the teacher's desk.

"Oh, wait, I need to get my book. I left it over there." Reuben points to a row of exercise books stacked on a shelf at the front of the classroom. He walks over to it as Joseph waits. As he walks past the bin he glances into it and sees half a sandwich lying in the bottom. *It must have been the remains of Mr Gately's lunch.* Reuben realises. *Wow, Joseph must really be hungry if he is taking food out of bins.*

He catches up with Joseph and they leave the classroom together. Joseph is very quiet now.

Go to 13.

72.

"If I put labels on everything that belongs to me then Joseph and his family will know which are my things. I'll do it now," Reuben says confidently. He marches off before anyone can say anything.

He grabs some paper and a pen and begins tearing it into pieces. He writes 'Reuben' on every piece of paper then he starts looking for the Sellotape.

Mrs Sense finds him. "Reuben, what on earth are you doing? I didn't think you were serious when you said that. Sit down for a minute, please. We need to talk."

"But Mum, I need to do this quickly before they arrive," Reuben answers.

"Oh, Reuben!" Mrs Sense is frustrated. "You

have a lot of nice things but where did they come from?"

"From you, from friends and family and some I saved up and bought with my own money." Reuben has no idea what his mother is talking about.

"Right, and your own money. Where did that come from?" Mrs Sense is patient as she waits for Reuben to understand.

"You, and people I did jobs for." Reuben remembers getting a pound for sweeping some leaves for one of their neighbours.

"Okay, Reuben. Who created us and everything in this world?" Mrs Sense hopes Reuben will see the connection.

Reuben looks confused. "God?" he asks.

"Yes, Reuben. So, who do all your things, including your money, really belong to?" Mrs Sense continues.

"God, I guess. Is that because He allows me to have them?" Reuben is finally starting to understand.

"Yes, he gives all good gifts. He also watches what we do with them. Do you think that God would want you to make sure that Joseph can't touch any of your things?" Mrs Sense gets to the main point.

"Well, if they are really God's things then

He would probably want me to share them. It's just so hard, Mum. I don't want my things to get damaged or lost." Reuben knows what he should do now. He starts tearing up the pieces of paper.

"If we are generous with our things and our money, God promises to bless us. Even if we don't get more money or things, we will receive a reward from God when we get to heaven. That's what we can look forward to," Mrs Sense carries on.

Reuben is already thinking about something else. He understands the main point though.

Go to 114.

73.

Reuben thinks back to when he was new at school. He didn't get invited to very many parties then. It's taken him a long time to make friends and to become popular at school. He thinks Joseph and every other child needs to do the same thing. They all need to work hard to make friendships with others. Why should he make it easier for Joseph when no one made it easier for him?

He decides not to invite Joseph and focuses instead on his main group of friends. He knows some people will be disappointed but that's just life.

The next day at school he hands out the few invitations and avoids Joseph and the others that he hasn't invited. They soon find out that they haven't been invited as all the other children are talking about it. Joseph looks really sad but doesn't say anything.

Reuben's party is on Saturday and there are only a few days to go. He is excited. He is surprised that he hasn't received more replies from people saying they are coming but he doesn't worry about it. He decides that people have just forgotten to write back.

On Friday, Billy, a popular boy in Reuben's class, comes up to him. Reuben isn't really friends with him as they have different groups but Billy has always been nice to Reuben. Reuben wonders what he wants.

"Hey Reuben, I'm really sorry about my party clashing with yours. My parents couldn't find another date as we will be away, so tomorrow was the only time we could do it. I hope it doesn't ruin your plans," Billy finishes.

"Oh, I didn't even know about your party," Reuben says. Things are suddenly starting to make sense now.

"I didn't invite you or Jack and Todd as I know they are your close friends. I know you have friends outside school from church and things, so I thought you would still have plenty of people attending your party. I also wanted to make sure everyone had somewhere to go so I invited the whole class." Billy seems cheerful and is acting as if it is not a big problem.

"Thanks for telling me Billy," Reuben backs away. He doesn't know what to do and feels like cancelling his party now.

Go to 98.

74.

Reuben writes out his invitations including everyone in his class. However, he suddenly realises that it will be the only time of the year when he will be given money to save up to buy some books that he really wants. He decides to make sure that this is what happens. As it is his birthday and he loves food, he wants as much as possible at his party.

He adds a note to the bottom of each invitation.

"Please bring at least £10 and some food to share. I will collect this at the door as I welcome you to my party."

Reuben signs all of the invitations and puts them in the envelopes. He tells his mum that the invitations are ready in the kitchen and he goes to bed.

Later in the evening, Mr and Mrs Sense are curious. Mrs Sense had been expecting Reuben to come and show her one of the invitations as he is usually very excited to show her things he has written or made. He hadn't done this and now she wonders what exactly he has written to his friends. She wants to protect Reuben from making serious mistakes that could damage his friendships but also wants him to learn some things for himself. His party is a big event, however, so Reuben's parents decide they will open one of the invitations to see what he has written.

Mrs Sense begins to read and Mr Sense looks over her shoulder. She starts off by saying, "Yes, that's good. He's explained what will be happening and given the address and time."

Mr Sense gasps as he reads the note at the bottom of the page. "Oh, no, Reuben!" he says.

"What? What has he done?....Oh, dear." Mrs Sense reaches the note at the end as well.

"Why would he write that?" Mr Sense asks.

"I think he wants to make sure that people know what's expected of them if they want to come to his party. It's just greed." Mrs Sense says. "At least, I hope it's that and not that he's trying to stop the poorer children from coming, that would be a lot worse."

Mr Sense looks thoughtful. "I hope it's not that as well. It would be awful to have a son who excludes people because they are poor. I hoped he had learned better than that at church and in Sunday School."

"I guess we had better talk to him about this tomorrow." Mrs Sense says.

Whoops! That didn't go very well, did it? Let's take Reuben back to the point that he is making decisions about who to invite and try again. *Go to 44Q.*

75.

Reuben realises that he *can* help Joseph. There are always people in his village needing things doing. He wouldn't get much money but it would be a start.

"Let's go now and see if we can find some jobs for you. There's dog walking, collecting newspapers, washing cars, tidying sheds...." Reuben lists all of the things he has thought of in the past when doing odd jobs for his mum. "My mum might pay you for some jobs as well," Reuben offers.

Joseph isn't sure. He doesn't really want Reuben to be this involved but it would be easier if two of them looked for work. After a few seconds, he nods.

"Let's go then," Reuben says and the two of them head off towards the village.

They spend the next hour walking around together knocking on doors and offering to do odd jobs for the local people. Some of the older people don't answer their doors as they have been taught not to by their relatives and friends. A few people offer them very low paid jobs in their gardens—sweeping leaves or tidying up.

Most of the people in the village are concerned about the age of these two boys and that their parents are allowing them to roam the village looking for work. They don't recognise one of the boys but the other one is known locally!

Finally, Mrs Jessop steps in and calls Mrs Sense, "Hello, Mrs Sense?"

"Yes, who's that? Oh, hello, Mrs Jessop, is everything okay?" Mrs Sense wonders why her neighbour would be calling. "Is this about Reuben? Where is he?" She puts two and two together and her young son is the only thing she can think of.

"Well, he's actually going around the village with another boy. They are knocking on doors and asking for work. I was worried that an older person might call the police in the end. Do you know what this is about?" Mrs Jessop is obviously curious.

"Oh dear, no I don't. I wondered where Reuben had got to. I'd best go out and find him. Where did you last see him?" Mrs Sense knows that she needs to find Reuben straight away before the police are called.

"Could you do me a big favour and pop over and watch the other kids whilst I head out?" she asks Mrs Jessop.

"Yes, of course. I'll be there in a second." Mrs Jessop is keen to help as she is worried about the boys.

Go to 99.

76.

Reuben wishes his mum wasn't always so direct. He is embarrassed that instead of thinking about what to do, she wants to pray! He worries what Joseph will think, maybe he will decide that the whole Sense family are religious....

Go to 78.

77.

Reuben is frustrated. Why can't his mum see

that it's time for action, not prayer! He wants to do something now! He is about to make a fuss but Joseph suddenly speaks up.

Go to 78.

78.

To Reuben's surprise, Joseph says, "Yes, I think that praying might be a good idea."

Joseph hasn't had much time for God in the past and the people he knows that are Christians don't often behave like it. "My family has never been interested in God, but I suppose it couldn't hurt to pray and then if God is there maybe he will help us."

Reuben follows Joseph's logical explanation. He has never thought of things in this way. How strange to grow up thinking that God might not even be there. He is pleased that his parents have taught him the truth from the Bible already. He decides that praying first is definitely the right option.

Mrs Sense looks pleased. "Right, let's pray." They sit down around the kitchen table. "Lord, please help us know what to do for Joseph's family. I pray that they might have somewhere to live. I pray that they might have food to eat and clothes to wear. Please lead and guide us as we make decisions about what to do next. I pray as well that they might know that you love and care for them. Thankyou Jesus for dying on the cross for our sin. I pray in Jesus Name. Amen."

She finishes her prayer and looks up. Joseph has his eyes closed and is definitely taking things seriously. Joseph is actually wondering about some of the things Mrs Sense has said in her prayer, but he keeps quiet about it for now.

"I think I should come with you to meet your mum. Would that be okay, Joseph? We can go and get back before dinner," Mrs Sense suggests carefully.

"Is that what God told you to do?" Joseph asks.

"Well God didn't tell me to do anything specifically. Now that we have prayed, though, we can be sure that he is leading us as we move forward." Mrs Sense wants to keep any explanations simple for now. "Shall we go, I can ask Mrs Jessop one of our neighbours to watch the other children for a bit. In fact, Reuben, can you just pop over and ask if she can do that? You can take Joseph with you as well." Mrs Sense doesn't want to lose any time now that she has made a decision. She wants the boys out of the house for a few minutes as well so she can call her husband.

She calls Mr Sense and explains her plan.

He is also keen to help the family in any way they can.

Go to 100.

79.

Poor Mr Jack had been hoping that Reuben wouldn't suggest this. Usually, he would have been happy to take Mrs Kline and her two children back to his farmhouse. His wife definitely wouldn't have minded. However, there is a very particular reason why he can't do this at the moment and it's not something he wants to explain to the children.

"I'm sorry, Reuben, I really can't do that right now. We have someone else staying with us, you see?" Mr Jack looks at Mrs Kline as if to say sorry.

Reuben looks so disappointed. "Can't you fit them in as well? You've always had lots of visitors before." Reuben doesn't realise he is being rude. He just really wants to help Joseph and his family.

"Reuben, I'm sorry, we can't do it this time. I'll tell you what though, Mrs Kline. I'm going to come back to see you again and maybe there will be something that can be done." Mr Jack looks thoughtful. "Please don't go anywhere for the time being."

"Okay, but don't trouble yourself. We're really okay here and it's just for a short time. We don't need any charity." Mrs Kline knows she is repeating herself but these people don't seem to be listening.

"Right, Reuben and Ellie. Let's go now," Mr Jack tells them firmly.

"What, we are just going to leave them?" Reuben can't believe it.

"For now, yes Reuben. Let's go please." Mr Jack wishes he could explain his reasons to Reuben so that he will understand but he needs to do some checks first.

Ellie climbs out of the tent and says goodbye to Jessica. The two children follow the big farmer back towards the Sense's house.

Go to 101.

80.

"Mr Jack," Reuben whispers, or at least he had thought it was a whisper but actually it was very loud. "I think the police should sort this out. They have houses and stuff, don't they?"

Mr Jack looks at Mrs Kline who has gone a pale colour at the mention of the police. "I don't think that's necessary in this case, Reuben.

Maybe Mrs Kline wants to stay here in peace. The police can't always help and they may just make things worse. This is also my land, so it's up to me whether they are allowed to stay here and until we have a better option, it's best for them to just stay here."

"I need to sort a few things out. Can we visit again tomorrow and make sure things are still okay?" Mr Jack says to Mrs Kline.

"Yes, but we really don't need all this fuss. Things will be sorted out soon and then we will be gone." Mrs Kline is embarrassed by the attention.

"Just please don't leave the area for now. I need to talk to you about something else." Mr Jack is trying not to sound strange but there is something Reuben doesn't know.

They say goodbye to Mrs Kline and Jessica and head back towards the Sense's house.

Go to 101.

81.

Reuben has definitely been reading too many adventure books. He decides they can handle the situation on their own.

The two boys take the food Reuben has gathered to the tent. Joseph opens the tent and the smell hits Reuben in the face. He looks in quickly and changes his mind. Joseph's mum and sister look seriously ill and he knows they need medical help straight away.

Go to 82

82.

Reuben knows that the nearest place from which to make a phone call is Mr Jack's farmhouse. "Wait here, I'm going to go and call an ambulance," he says. "Oh and you might want to pray for them whilst you're waiting," he calls as he leaves.

"But, I'm not religious," Joseph answers. Then, he decides that praying might work as there is nothing else to do. He sits down and tries to think of a good prayer.

Reuben runs as fast as he can. He arrives at the front door of the Jacks' farmhouse red in the face and struggling to breathe. Mrs Jack answers the door.

"Mrs Jack, please call an ambulance, there are some sick people in a tent near the wood in your field." Reuben doesn't realise that this won't make much sense to anyone who doesn't know the whole story.

"What?! Reuben calm down and let's talk

about this. Oh, hello, Patrick,." She greets a man that has just walked into the room. "Young Reuben here says there are some people in a tent and they need an ambulance, I'm just trying to get to the bottom of his story."

Reuben looks at the man. He feels like he has seen him somewhere but he isn't sure where exactly. "Who are you?" he asks.

"Patrick Kline, who are you?" the man responds.

"Reuben Sense."

"Reuben, who are the people in the tent and why do they need an ambulance?" Mrs Jack wants to refocus the conversation.

"Joseph is a school friend of mine and he's with his mum and sister. They've been living in a tent but they are very ill, I think it might be from drinking dirty water," Reuben rushes the words.

"That sounds like my family!" Patrick nearly shouts. "Where are they?" he demands.

Reuben looks at Mrs Jack as Mr Jack joins them. "What's going on?" the big farmer asks.

Mrs Jack explains things to her husband and gets on the phone to call an ambulance, just in case there is really an emergency.

Mr Jack takes control. "Right, Reuben, Patrick. Let's go. We'll make sure the ambulance staff know where the tent is when we get there." He shouts the last comment to his wife as they leave the house.

The three of them rush through the fields and along pathways until they reach the tent area. Joseph is waiting, he looks like he is panicking.

"How are they now?" Patrick shouts as he nearly breaks down the tent entrance in trying to get to his wife and daughter. "Oh, no! The ambulance needs to get here quickly."

Joseph looks stunned. He hasn't seen his father for quite a few months. "Dad, what happened? Why are you here? Where have you been? I thought you left us." Joseph starts to cry.

Patrick turns away from the tent and towards his son. "No, I didn't leave you by choice. You have to trust me for now. I promise I will explain later. We all need to be strong to get through this together, okay?"

"Okay, Dad." Joseph tries to put on a brave face.

Reuben watches the scene not really knowing what to do. Mr Jack walks up and down hoping the ambulance will arrive quickly. There are sirens in the distance. "I'll go and direct them," Reuben shouts. He runs off before anyone can stop him. He needs a break from the whole situation anyway!

He reaches the road and waits for the ambulance to arrive. It pulls up alongside him. "Yes, they are through here in this field," he tells the man and woman that climb out of the vehicle with their equipment.

"Do you know what's wrong with them?" they ask Reuben.

"Someone said something about drinking water from the stream but I'm not sure really," Reuben says.

"Okay, lead the way," the man instructs.

They follow Reuben through the woods and it isn't long before they reach the tent. After a quick examination, they load Mrs Kline onto a stretcher and Mr Kline is asked if he can carry his daughter to the ambulance.

Everyone sets off back towards the ambulance. When they get there, Mr Kline and Joseph ride in the back with the ambulance staff.

"They will be okay, we got to them in time. It looks like they are suffering from drinking dirty water and then not having enough good water to replace it during their sickness. You did a good job in getting help," the lady ambulance person tells Reuben as she shuts the back doors. The ambulance speeds away with sirens blaring.

Reuben turns to Mr Jack. "Right, let's get you home then young Reuben. I think you'll have a lot of explaining to do to your parents!"

They head over to the Sense's house. Reuben tells the story to his mum and dad. They tell him off for not asking for their help earlier on but are relieved that everyone is okay.

Patrick stays with his family in the hospital whilst they are recovering. Joseph learns that his father has actually been in prison after making some bad choices in his business and losing all the family's money. Joseph is sad but thinks that this is better than if he had left them!

Patrick tells them that he is really sorry and that he has changed but he knows it will take time to prove it to them. He explains how the Jack's had found him sleeping in a field and had taken him in. Then, he had gone to church with them and after a few weeks had become a Christian. Now, he wants his family to see what a difference Jesus has made in his life giving him a new hope and purpose. He shows them his new Bible and reads a few verses to them.

The government manage to find a house for the family to move into whilst they are in the hospital. They will stay in the area and Mrs Kline is willing to go to church with her husband. Joseph also wants to go, he remembers the prayer that he prayed when he was really in need and how God helped his family and brought them back together.

Reuben is pleased that Joseph will be staying as he now has a new friend at school. He has learned lessons about trying to do too much by himself though. What if the family had become seriously ill and died because he thought he could handle things alone? He decides that next time, he will ask his parents for help....

Go to 111

83.

They walk over to the tent and wake Jessica. Then the whole group head over to the Jacks' house.

When they all arrive, Mrs Jack opens the door, then takes a big breath as she sees the large number of people on her doorstep. "Well, I guess you'd better come in...and the police as well? Oh my! Who wants tea?" She doesn't know what to say and decides that tea is always a good idea.

"Can we all gather around first because I need to get back to my duties?" PC Sansing makes the polite request.

"Yes, of course. Let's gather here in the lounge," Mr Jack suggests.

Mrs Kline gasps as her husband suddenly appears from one of the other rooms. Joseph also looks surprised but he has had a little time already to prepare himself. Jessica screams, "Daddy!" and runs into his arms. Patrick hugs her and turns to face the rest of them.

"I hope you can all manage to work things

out here. I'm not going to be taking any action against these young lads for knocking on doors and asking for work. I know they were just trying to help."

PC Sansing turns to Reuben and Joseph, "Boys, in future, get an adult involved, don't try to handle things yourself as you might get into serious trouble."

The officer moves to Patrick and offers his hand. "Good to see you out of trouble. I heard there have been some changes in your life that should mean you keep on the straight and narrow?"

"Yes, I'm following Jesus now. I realised that what I did before was wrong and that I need to be an example to my family and lead them properly. I intend to do that now if they will give me another chance." Mr Kline looks towards his wife hoping that she is willing.

Mrs Kline moves towards him and stands by his side. Joseph smiles a little and nods, he will follow his mother's lead.

PC Sansing leaves the house.

"Right, I know we have a lot of talking to do but I think this is a good time to tell you that the government has found us somewhere to live already," Mr Kline announces. "The problem before was that after I was released from prison I didn't have a fixed place where I could receive letters. Since the Jacks' let me stay with them, I've been working on finding somewhere and the department phoned today to tell me they have a place for us. Shall we go and see it?" Mr Kline looks at his wife standing next to him. She leans against him looking like she might faint, but she is smiling.

Mrs Jack gets her some water. "It's just such good news, I don't know if it's real," she says.

"Where is the new place?" Mrs Sense asks. She looks at Reuben.

"Don't worry, we will be staying in this area." Mr Kline guesses the reason for the question as he can see that Joseph wants to keep Reuben as a friend.

"Yes!" Reuben and Joseph high-five. Mrs Sense is hopeful that Ellie might be a good friend for Jessica as well. She is thrilled that Patrick has become a Christian already.

They all thank the Jacks' and go to look at the Kline's new house. After a quick look around, Reuben and Mrs Sense leave the Kline family to their reunion.

Reuben has learned some lessons that he won't forget and intends to keep Joseph as one of his very best friends.

Go to 111.

84.

"Oh hello, Sir, sorry, I was just trying to find my ball. It went into this hedge from the other side." Reuben jumps out of the hedge to face the man and moves away from the yapping dog. The dog moves along and soon has Joseph jumping out of the hedge as well.

"I suppose there were two balls...were there?" the man says. "Let's have the truth now from one of you, please." The old man wasn't born yesterday and there are no balls to be seen.

Reuben tries again, "Really, Sir, I don't know this kid. He looks like he's from the poor part of town, don't you think? I'm telling the truth but I have no idea where he came from."

"Then whose book is this?" The man holds the book up.

Reuben swallows. He wants so much to claim his special book but he knows that if he does then he is admitting that he wasn't just searching for his ball.

"It's mine," Joseph speaks up and glares at Reuben. "I was just walking past and saw your swing. I thought it looked like a nice place to read and as I'm from the poor part of town I don't have anywhere else to go."

The man looks like he might be feeling sorry for Joseph. "My wife and I often help the poor kids at church. Why don't you come in and have some juice and biscuits with us? You can tell us about the story you've been reading. I would like to be reminded of it, bring back my youth!"

Reuben stares at the man and Joseph. He is speechless. "What about me?" he whines.

"I thought you had a ball to find, best you get on with searching for it," the man says. He puts his arm around Joseph's shoulder and walks him towards the house with Reuben's book! Joseph turns briefly and sticks his tongue out at Reuben as he walks away.

Reuben heads home. He has lost his books, got into trouble and lost Joseph as a friend by making up stories and trying to get Joseph into trouble.

Joseph hangs around with other children at school from this point on and Reuben loses his chance to be a friend to him. If he wants to try again and make different choices. He needs to return to the beginning of the story. <u>Go to 1.</u>

85.

It's party day. Reuben is very excited. Everything has been arranged and he just has to wait for his classmates and others to arrive. The bouncy castle has been set up in the garden and the trampoline nearby. There are craft activities and party bags for everyone to take home. Reuben is also excited about the presents he will receive and the food his mum has made. Ellie, Toby and Noah are also excited and don't understand that the party is not for them! Dodgy their dog is running back and forth and licking everyone.

The doorbell rings. Jack and Todd are some of the first to arrive. They are Reuben's closest friends. Daniel a newer friend from the poorer part of town also arrives. The boys head off into the garden to play. Other children arrive over the next half hour until everybody is here, except Joseph.

Joseph arrives late and he is on his own. All of the other children have been brought by their parents. Some of the adults are hanging around and chatting to assist with supervising the party and maybe so they can make sure their children are safe. Joseph isn't carrying anything and is dressed in the same type of ragged clothes that he wore to school on his first day. His hair looks cleaner though and he doesn't look too dirty.

Reuben isn't around so Mrs Sense welcomes him. She hopes that Reuben will at least spend some time with him.

Joseph wanders into the garden where all of the other children are playing with each other.

"Why don't you have a go at this?" Mrs Sense says to him. She has followed him out to make sure he is included.

She is pointing to a game where you have to throw hoops over a stick stuck upright in the ground from a distance. Reuben and quite a few of the other children are lining up to play and it is getting very competitive. There is a lot of shouting and shrieking after each person's turn.

"Okay, yes, I can do that," Joseph says quietly and lines up to take his turn.

"Oh, hi, Joseph," Reuben says. He knows that he will beat most of the others at the game but he isn't sure about Joseph as he is new. "Are you good at this?"

"I don't know, I've never tried it before," Joseph says.

Reuben has his turn and gets a good score. He is in the lead and sure that he will win the game and get the small prize that will be awarded.

Joseph takes his turn and misses with the first hoop.

"Oh, bad luck," Reuben says. Secretly he is pleased though as he really wants to win.

"Wait, Reuben, he still has two more shots," Mrs Sense reminds her son. She hopes that someone will beat Reuben as it's not good for him to win every time.

"I'm not sure that I can do any better," Joseph says as he takes his next turn. He throws the hoop which ends up around the highest score.

"Wow," the other children are gathering around now to watch his final throw.

"If you can do that again, you will win," someone says to Joseph.

"I don't think I can though," he says nervously. He throws the final hoop in exactly the same way that he threw the second one. It lands in the same spot and he wins the game.

"Very well done, Joseph," Mrs Sense is the first the congratulate him. "Well, Reuben, aren't you pleased for Joseph?"

85Q. What will Reuben say?

A. "Well done, Joseph, Good shot." *Go to 102.*

B. "I wanted to win." *Go to 103.*

C. "Did you bring me a present?" *Go to 104.*

86.

Reuben is just so curious that he keeps asking Joseph to let him see inside his house. He can't understand how Joseph can live in a house like this having turned up at school looking so dirty. The house looks expensive.

"Okay, I guess," Joseph replies. "I just need to search for this key as I'm not sure exactly where my mum left it."

The boys walk around the outside of the house and begin turning over plant pots and looking under stones and doormats. Reuben finally finds a single key that looks like it might be for a door. He hands it to Joseph. "Good that I was here, isn't it? Otherwise, you might still be looking and stuck outside!" Reuben feels pleased with himself.

"Yeah," Joseph says but he looks very worried.

"Reuben, maybe we should do this another day. I'm meant to ask if I want to have visitors." Joseph sounds like he is afraid of his parents but this just makes Reuben more curious.

"Come on, let's go in. I can leave before your parents get back if you're worried, or I can just hide and then go out of the window if we hear them." Reuben is starting to enjoy this. It's like an adventure in one of his books.

"Okay, I think it's this door," Joseph says as he leads Reuben around to the back of the house. He puts the key in the lock and turns it. The door opens and Joseph tiptoes in.

A small dog comes rushing towards them

growling. Joseph backs away and tries to shut the door again but the dog is standing guarding the entrance and is snarling at them.

"What's your dog's name? It doesn't seem very friendly," Reuben says.

"Um, Stoney," Joseph says looking at the stones on the ground.

"Weird," Reuben replies but doesn't have time to think much more about it as the dog is out of the house and running down the drive.

Joseph pulls Reuben into the house and slams the door quickly. 'Stoney' is still outside.

"Wait, aren't you going to get your dog?" Reuben asks.

"No, he's alright outside," Joseph says. He leads Reuben upstairs. "Come and have a look….at my room." Joseph finishes the sentence as he leads Reuben into a child's room.

There are toys and games around and Reuben sees boy's clothes hanging up in the wardrobe. Now, he is very confused. Why is Joseph wearing rags when he has nice, clean clothes to choose from?

Joseph sits down on the bed and places Reuben's books beside him. He seems awkward and uncomfortable. "What shall we do then?" he asks Reuben.

"What do you think?" Reuben asks.

There is a noise outside. Joseph jumps up

and rushes to a window. "Oh no," he says. "You need to get out of here, my parents are home."

"Are you sure they won't want to meet me?" Reuben asks. He can't believe that any parents could be so rude to their children's friends.

"No, they really won't. Let's go." Joseph is firm.

They rush downstairs and head for the back door. There are noises just outside and a shadow behind the door.

"Quick, this way." Joseph drags Reuben across the lounge towards the front door. They hear voices.

"Chappy, how did you get outside?" A woman's voice and then a dog barking.

"That's really very strange. Thank goodness he didn't run off. Do you think you forgot to shut him in the house after his walk earlier?" A man is speaking now.

"Oh, look, the door is already open! You'd better call the police." The woman sounds scared. "Go on Chappy, you can check if anyone is here."

The dog goes running off around the house as the two boys try to get the front door open. "I thought you said his name was Stoney? You don't live here, do you?" Reuben whispers to Joseph. He is terrified.

They finally get the door open but Chappy jumps up and bites Reuben's arm then he catches

Reuben's trouser leg in his teeth and hangs on. Reuben yells.

Joseph runs off down the drive towards the road leaving Reuben struggling with the small yapping dog.

86Q. What will Reuben do?

A. Take the dog with him if necessary. <u>Go to 105.</u>

B. Tell the old couple who he is and what he is doing. <u>Go to 106.</u>

C. Make up a story. <u>Go to 107.</u>

87.

"Okay, I'm going home then." Reuben knows that if he really wants this friendship to last, he needs to give Joseph time and not be too pushy. He thinks it's a bit odd that Joseph is living in such a big house but wearing rags to school.

He walks home and tells his mum everything. "You know mum, I'm sure he's living in the house we visited once. Did the old people there have children or grandchildren?" Reuben is trying to figure out the mystery.

Mrs Sense looks thoughtful. "Reuben, I saw

the Chuckson's recently and they still live there. I don't think they have any children. Are you sure it was the same house?"

"Pretty sure, yes," Reuben wonders what is going on.

"You know, I think we need to pray for Joseph and his family as it sounds like there's more to this story that we don't know yet." Mrs Sense detects something that Reuben is too young to understand.

"Maybe you could invite Joseph to your party Reuben and get to know him a bit better?" Mrs Sense suggests.

"I might do, but I want to make sure he looks after my books first. I'm worried that he might damage them." Reuben doesn't realise how unimportant this is.

"Okay Reuben, well, it's your decision, but remember that I can always replace your books." Mrs Sense wants Reuben to be Joseph's friend and to find out if his family really need help.

Go to 61.

88.

This is Reuben's adventure and I guess an eight-year-old boy is likely to choose the spying option more often than someone else.

Reuben says goodbye and pretends to leave. He then cuts back and buries himself in the hedge that surrounds the big house. He can see through into the driveway area.

He waits for a while and watches Joseph as he hangs around. Joseph then walks down to the garden shed and sits on a swing that is nearby. He gets one of Reuben's books out and starts reading it.

Reuben feels a bit annoyed as *he* would like to be at his home reading but he is having to spy on Joseph. Joseph is now in the middle of an adventure by reading one of Reuben's books!

Reuben waits for a while. It feels like ages to a young boy, but it's probably only thirty minutes or so. Joseph laughs out loud a few times as he moves through the book. He is a fast reader and Reuben is surprised.

Suddenly, a car is heard on the road and before anyone can move, it swings into the driveway of the house. A dog starts barking in the house.

Joseph jumps up as if he has forgotten where he is. Reuben expects him to rush and greet his family arriving home, but instead, he dives into the hedge just a little bit further along than Reuben is. He leaves Reuben's book on the swing!

Reuben holds his breath realising that

Joseph obviously doesn't live in this house and that they are both now hiding in the hedge of a garden that doesn't belong to either of them.

The barking gets louder and a small dog is rushing towards them. Reuben hears voices.

"What is it Chappy?" a man's voice.

"Squirrels again probably," says a woman who sounds bored.

"I don't think so, he is making a right noise and heading for the hedge area." The man starts following the dog towards the hedge.

Reuben realises that he will be the first to be found as he is nearer to the dog.

The man catches sight of the swing which is still moving from Joseph's quick exit. "What's this?" The man walks over and picks up Reuben's book. "*The Adventurous Four* by Enid Blyton. I haven't read one of these since I was a boy." The man looks around trying to solve the mystery of the book on the swing.

Chappy is sniffing the hedge near Reuben and finally gets hold of his T-shirt sleeve and won't let go. "Ouch, ouch." Reuben starts to cry and panic.

"Who's there?" the man asks, "And what are you doing in my hedge?"

88Q. *What will Reuben say?*

A. Tell the man why he is there. *Go to 112.*

B. Make up a story. *Go to 84.*

89.

"I can't lend you any more books, Joseph. My mum won't be happy if they get damaged. Do you know how to get to the library?" Reuben feels a bit guilty as he has hundreds of books and it's only one that's been damaged but he can't deal with further damage. He loves his books!

Joseph looks so sad. "I don't have a library card yet," he says.

"It's easy to get one, you just need to take an adult with you then give your name and address. It's free." Reuben thinks he is being helpful.

"Okay, thanks, Reuben. Maybe I'll try that."

Reuben notices after this that Joseph seems to stay away from him and hang around with some of the other children. He wonders what he can do instead of lending Joseph his books to show that he still wants to be friends.

His birthday is coming up, he decides to invite Joseph.

Go to 56.

90.

Reuben is so upset about his book being damaged that he bursts into tears.

Mr Gately comes over, "What on earth's the matter, Reuben?" he asks.

"I lent Joseph one of my favourite books and he's ruined it," Reuben whines as he continues sobbing. "I knew this would happen as he's poor and dirty, but I was trying to be kind."

"Reuben, that's enough. How do you think Joseph feels. I'm sure he didn't do it on purpose." Mr Gately knows that Reuben's family has more than enough money to replace the book. He guesses from what he has seen so far that Joseph's family are very poor.

Joseph looks devastated and just stands there. He had been grinning as he talked about the adventure. The damage to the book hadn't looked that bad when he had brought it to school. Now, he wishes he hadn't borrowed anything from Reuben in the first place.

He decides to stay well away from Reuben and to make other friends in the class.

It looks like Reuben has made his mind up about Joseph and doesn't want to be friends with him really. If he had wanted to, he should've known that books and other things are not as important as people. He also missed the chance to tell Joseph about God and to invite him to church as he was too busy worrying about his books. If he wants to make different decisions. He will need to start this book again. Go to 1.

91.

"It's great that you enjoyed the adventure," Reuben says. He manages to ignore the fact that his book is damaged as he knows his mum will replace it and that his friendship with Joseph is more important.

"Really, it's okay?" Joseph says. He seems relieved. He had seen the shock on Reuben's face when he gave him back his book.

"Yes, no problem. I will bring you the next ones. Maybe you can find somewhere safe to read them," Reuben jokes and Joseph laughs.

"Great, I wanted to talk to you about one of the stories I read. Do you have time after school?" Joseph asks. He waits for the answer. He is a little shy.

"Yes, we can walk home together if you like?" Reuben asks.

"Okay, that sounds good. Actually, I wanted to ask you some things anyway." Joseph is starting to trust Reuben.

The boys get to the end of the school day

and begin walking home together. They talk about adventures and have a great time comparing their own stories that they have made up. Reuben realises that Joseph thinks in the same way that he does and that they could be good friends.

"Reuben, I really need to tell someone some things about my family, but I'm afraid. Can I trust you?" Joseph suddenly says.

Reuben doesn't know what to say. He is worried about making a promise he won't be able to keep but he does want to be a good friend to Joseph. He sends up a quick prayer to God asking for Him to help him make this important decision.

"Is your family in some kind of trouble with the police?" he asks.

"No, it's not that. It's more awkward and embarrassing really," Joseph says.

Reuben notices that he has walked past the turning that he needs to take to go home. He decides that listening to Joseph is more important for now. He is also very curious by this point. They continue walking along a path that seems to be heading into the woods towards land owned by Mr Jack, the local farmer.

"Let's sit down here," Joseph suggests.

They sit on some tree stumps and Reuben waits for Joseph to speak. "It's like this. My family are living…."

There is a man's voice and it is very loud. "Joe, is that you?" The man approaches as the boys jump up.

"Dad?" Joseph says. He looks pale and a bit frightened. "How did you find us? Have you seen Mum?"

Reuben looks at the dirty middle-aged man standing in front of them. He looks as if he hasn't slept for quite a while and that he might be ill. "That's your dad?" Reuben asks the obvious question.

"Joe, I just need to talk to your mother and to you, to explain." The man is desperate but not moving forward anymore.

"But, you left us, I didn't think I would ever see you again. Where have you been?" Joseph starts crying and backing away.

Reuben doesn't know what to do. He tells the man, "I think you should leave. You're upsetting Joseph." He tries to be brave but he can't believe what he is hearing.

"Joe, I made a mistake, but I didn't leave you. I had no choice." The man is moving forward again.

"What do you mean? Of course, you had a choice. You could've stayed with us. We've been sleeping in a tent because of you," Joseph sobs but stands still. He decides to face his father as he has things he wants to say to him.

"No, Joe. I'm so sorry, but when the police took me away, they wouldn't even let me say goodbye. You kids were sleeping." Joseph's dad looks miserable.

"Police? What?" Reuben hears the word and looks at Joseph. "What is he talking about, do you know?"

"The police took you away? Why? Where have you been?" Joseph has a lot more questions now.

"I thought you knew. I went to prison. I made some bad decisions and the business went bankrupt." Joseph's father looks broken and so sad. It makes Reuben want to cry.

"You were in prison!? But Mum told us you just left!" Joseph is very confused and doesn't know who to believe.

"I think she probably wanted to protect you from the shame of what I did." Joseph's dad is pleading with his son to believe him.

"So, when did you get out?" Joseph calms down a little and wants some answers.

"About a month ago. I came looking for you all straight away and heard that there were some campers on this land. I came here to see if it was you as I knew you wouldn't have any money or anywhere to go. I'm so, so sorry." Joseph's dad seems to be telling the truth.

Reuben feels as if his head might explode. Police, prison, crime, people living in tents. These are all things that he cannot understand. His life is so normal and he is glad about it.

"Okay, so where have *you* been living?" Joseph asks.

"I was sleeping in fields here and there whilst I looked for you but then a farmer saw me one day and told me I could stay in his house. He and his wife have really been very kind. Joe, I've really changed, they even took me to church with them!" Joseph's dad has a sort of brightness about him as he speaks about church. He still looks dirty and tired but different in some way.

"That must be Mr and Mrs Jack. He owns all this land," Reuben tells him. "They are Christians."

"So, you've become religious?" Joseph looks like he can't believe it.

"Hey, Reuben, you're religious too, right?" Joseph focuses on his new friend for a second.

"I'm a Christian, yes," Reuben says and remembers his prayer just before Joseph's father came along.

"So, do you know where your mother is now?" Joseph's dad turns back to his son.

"Of course, I do, I need to ask her first whether she wants to see you though," Joseph says.

"Reuben could you just stay here a minute? The place we have been staying isn't far away and I need to go and talk to my mum quickly." Joseph turns to his new friend again.

91Q. What will Reuben decide?

A. He has helped Joseph enough already and just needs to go home. Go to 113.

B. To help him by staying with Joseph's father. Go to 108.

92.

"You know what, I'm bored of this adventure," Reuben tells Joseph. "I'm going home." He starts walking away.

Joseph stares after him with his mouth open. He can't believe that Reuben is behaving like a small child who says he wants something but then when he gets it he doesn't want it anymore.

Reuben continues walking but he is so busy thinking about what he is going to eat when he gets home that he doesn't see the leg of the man until he has tripped over it.

"Ouch, look where you're going will you…," the man says.

"Who are you?" Reuben asks as he jumps

back. The man is lying by the side of the path and had probably been asleep.

"I'm just here looking for my family. You must be about the same age as my Joe." The man looks at him. Reuben thinks that the man looks a bit like Joseph and he is also dirty and wearing ragged clothes. He keeps this to himself.

"I'm going home," he says sharply and continues on his way leaving the man looking after him.

Reuben had the chance to investigate this story and possibly have an adventure but he has chosen not to by going home in the middle of it. Such a shame! He won't find out who the man really is and what has happened to Joseph unless he starts again and makes different decisions. <u>Go to 1.</u>

93.

"I don't lend my books," Reuben answers. Todd looks disappointed. "You lent them to me," he says quietly as Daniel waits for him.

"Yes, but you are my friend. Daniel is, well, he's different." Reuben doesn't know how to explain it but he feels sure that Todd will understand.

"No, actually, Reuben. You're the one who

is different or at least, you should be. I thought you were a Christian?"

"I am," Reuben says. He doesn't see what that has to do with lending books.

"Aren't you meant to be kind to others and share things with them?" Todd asks him.

"Oh….," Reuben suddenly realises.

"I think you should probably go home and come to my house another time Reuben. I don't like your attitude towards Daniel and I think you need to sort things out with God before you do anything else." Todd is upset and feels bad for Daniel who has listened to the whole discussion.

"Let's go, Daniel," Todd says.

Reuben can't think of anything to say. He knows that Todd is right and that he has been unfair to Daniel.

That was pretty selfish of Reuben. Surely it wouldn't have cost him that much to lend one of his books to someone who doesn't seem to have anything? How does God feel about Reuben's behaviour? Reuben has also missed the chance to show Daniel that he cares about him. Daniel may have become a good friend of Reuben's but not now!

Reuben needs to spend some time thinking about this and if he wants to change his attitude then he will need to start the book again! *Go to 1.*

94.

"There you are Daniel, I knew he would say yes. Reuben is a generous kid."

The three boys walk together towards Todd's house. Reuben finds that he has a lot in common with Daniel due to their love of reading. Daniel's family can't afford to buy him books of his own but he spends a lot of time at the public library. Reuben is amazed that Daniel is quite clever. He had assumed that he wasn't as he never said much in class.

They get to Todd's house and he asks his mum to call Reuben's mum. She does it straight away and Mrs Sense agrees that Reuben can stay for tea.

The three boys play games and Reuben tells them about his birthday party. They have a great evening and then it is time for Reuben and Daniel to leave.

"You can borrow my books anytime you like," Reuben says to Daniel as they walk down the path. "I hope we can also be friends."

"I'd like that," Daniel says. "Maybe you'd like to come to church with me sometime?"

Reuben can't believe it. Daniel goes to church? "Are you a Christian then?" he asks.

"Yes, and I'd really like you to come to my

church Sunday School group," Daniel says.

Reuben feels very guilty, he knows he judged Daniel for all the wrong reasons. He was worried about him being poor but now Daniel is trying to share his faith with him. Daniel is behaving like a real Christian should!

"Daniel, I'm really sorry that I haven't really spoken to you before. I'm actually a Christian too," Reuben admits.

Daniel looks surprised but quickly accepts what Reuben has said. "That's great! We can go to Sunday School together."

"I'd like that and I'm also going to invite all of our class to my birthday party. I hope you will be able to come?" Reuben asks.

"I hope so too," Daniel answers as the boys head in different directions to their houses.

Go to 56.

95.

Mrs Kline, Joseph and Jessica settle into the Sense's home. They have dinner as a big group and then the children go off to play. Reuben and Joseph read adventure stories together which is much more fun than doing it alone.

Mrs Sense knows that this is the time to talk to Mrs Kline about her husband. She makes her a cup of tea and they sit down to chat. The whole story spills out of Mrs Kline as she cries. Mrs Sense puts her arm around the poor lady.

"I don't know quite how to tell you this. I think it's best just to say it," she begins. "Your husband has been living at the Jacks' farm. Mr Jack found him sleeping in one of his fields and they took him in. He seems to want to sort himself out and has been going to their church with them." Mrs Sense waits for Mrs Kline's response, not sure whether to continue.

"Oh, wow. I don't know what to say. I didn't think he would have been released from prison yet. Do you really think he has changed?" Mrs Kline looks hopeful.

"Mr Jack seems to think he wants to." Mrs Sense doesn't want to give false hope but she does want to see the family back together.

"I guess you'll be wanting us out of your house as soon as possible....," Mrs Kline says.

"No, that's not what this is about. You can stay here as long as you need to, honestly." Mrs Sense tries to make her feel welcome.

Over the next months, the Sense family and the Jack family spend a lot of time together as they allow the Kline's to try and rebuild their family. The adults do a lot of talking about what went wrong and Mr Kline tries to show his family that he has really changed. They see him reading a Bible and praying at the start of every day. That seems to be a miracle by itself as he never did much reading or staying in one place before. He had always been too busy.

Mrs Kline has never had much time for religion but she sees Christianity in action in the lives of the families supporting her and starts to wonder about God.

Reuben and Joseph enjoy their adventures and spend a lot of time together at school. Ellie and Jessica also become good friends as they share stories about princesses.

Finally, the day comes when the Kline's are ready to move back in together. The government has provided a place for them to live and Mr Kline has found a job. They will be staying in the area. Reuben is thrilled that he will still have Joseph as a friend. They will have the chance to have many more adventures although hopefully not ones that get them into trouble!

Go to 111.

96.

Reuben immediately forgets his promise to Joseph. "Joseph was hungry and looking for food."

he states.

"In my bin?" asks Mr Gately looking towards Joseph.

"I guess so," Reuben says. "That's a bit disgusting, isn't it? I knew I couldn't be friends with him."

Mr Gately looks shocked. "Reuben that's not what I meant. If you were as hungry as Joseph obviously is, then you might be pleased to eat food from the bin as well. Your auntie lives in the Philippines, doesn't she? I'm sure she has talked to you about children having to eat from the rubbish bins…."

Reuben is silent as he knows that this is true. He can't imagine what it must be like as he always has more than enough food. He feels sorry for Joseph now.

Joseph has gone very red. "I'm sorry Mr Gately it won't happen again. I think I need to leave now."

He rushes out of the classroom before Mr Gately or Reuben can react. They follow him outside but he has already gone.

"Reuben, you really must be more aware of people's feelings. I know you were telling the truth and that is good, but…." Mr Gately doesn't know what to say. He can't really tell Reuben off as he did tell the truth.

"It's my fault. I just made a promise to

Joseph that I wouldn't tell anyone but then I told you straight away to get myself out of trouble. I guess I shouldn't make promises that I can't keep." Reuben realises that whatever he had done he would have been in difficulty after he had made the promise to keep Joseph's secret. It wasn't something he could deal with as a child by himself.

Let's take him back a few steps to see what happens if he makes different choices after Mr Gately asks him to be Joseph's friend. <u>*Go back to 15Q.*</u>

97.

"Okay boys, get home now then or your parents will be worried about you," Mr Gately instructs.

Joseph and Reuben head quickly out of the classroom. "Thanks so much," Joseph whispers to Reuben.

"It's okay but are you going to tell me what is going on now? Why are you so hungry and where do you live?" Reuben is suspicious.

"Okay, but please keep it to yourself. My dad left after he lost all our money. So, we've been living in a tent near a field," Joseph tells Reuben.

"What?!" Reuben really can't believe it. He definitely hadn't thought there would be a story like this behind Joseph's odd behaviour. "Look, I will try to help you. I can bring you food. Who are you living there with if your dad has gone?" Reuben tries to understand what Joseph is telling him.

"My mum and my younger sister," Joseph says. "The problem is, they are both ill. I think it might be from the lack of food and also the water from the stream near to our campsite. I don't really know what to do. I haven't been feeling that well today either," Joseph looks worried.

"Let me get you all some food. I will bring it later from my house, then we can talk a bit more. Where exactly is your tent?" Reuben is already planning his excuses for leaving his house to see Joseph later on.

Joseph gives him rough directions and they go their separate ways. Reuben hurries home thinking of how he can get enough food without his mum asking too many questions. He doesn't want to lie to her but he knows it might be difficult.

He has a little bit of money of his own. He wonders if that would be enough to buy some bread and a few things from the corner shop in the village.

He gets home and collects his money from

his tin. "I'm just going around to a friend's house," he says. "I'll be back in less than an hour." This isn't lying as he is going to see a friend but maybe a tent isn't really a house. He decides that it's close enough.

He goes straight to the corner shop and buys as many things as he can carry with his ten pounds and eighty nine pence.

Reuben follows the directions he was given by Joseph and finally sees the small pink tent next to one of Mr Jack's fields. Joseph is waiting nearby.

"How are your mum and sister?" Reuben asks as he drops his bags of groceries.

"Not well at all. I'm afraid it might be serious. What do you think we should do?" Joseph asks.

97Q. What will Reuben say?

A. Let's give them some food and see if they get better. Go to 81.

B. I think we should call an ambulance. Go to 82.

98.

Reuben has his party as planned but it is a

sad event. Only a few people turn up as they all go to Billy's party. The few people that Billy hasn't invited are annoyed with Reuben as they would rather have gone where everyone else is. Even Jack and Todd seem upset.

Maybe it wasn't such a good idea to exclude certain people? Shall we <u>go back to 44Q</u> and make that decision again?

99.

As soon as Mrs Jessop arrives, Mrs Sense is out of the door and off down the drive towards the area of the last sighting of Reuben and the other boy. She can't think why on earth Reuben would be asking people for work and can only guess that it has something to do with the other boy he is with.

As she approaches the area she sees a police car parked up on the verge.

"Oh no." Mrs Sense has been here before. There had been an incident a while before where Reuben nearly flooded his school and the police had been involved then as well. He was getting a bit of a reputation in the village.

Mrs Sense runs towards the police car and around the corner. Reuben and another boy are standing in the road talking to PC Sansing.

"We just needed to find a few odd jobs for Joseph," Reuben is explaining. "His family don't have enough food, so I thought I'd help them."

"Reuben, what on earth?" Mrs Sense arrives at the scene and is breathless from her run.

"Mum, this is my friend Joseph," Reuben says. He doesn't seem to realise that he is going to be in a lot of trouble or that he is already in a lot of trouble!

Joseph is standing quietly to one side.

PC Sansing turns to him. "Why are your family living in a tent? Where is your father?" he asks him gently.

"He left us when he lost all our money," Joseph explains.

"What is his name? I just need to run some checks." PC Sansing takes the name of Joseph's father and walks away to try and find out what's really going on.

"Oh, Reuben. Why didn't you just ask us to help Joseph?" Mrs Sense can't believe that the two boys have been trying to manage things by themselves.

"I don't know, Mum." Reuben says. "It seemed like we could sort it out, but no one wanted to give us odd jobs because we are too young."

"They probably thought you were going to steal things from their houses! Oh dear." Mrs

Sense thinks of the worst thing possible.

PC Sansing comes back. "Joseph, where did you say you've been sleeping? I mean, where's the tent?"

"I can't really explain, but I could show you." Joseph is relieved that someone else seems to want to help him. It has been a heavy burden for a young boy to try and carry.

"I need to talk to your mum. I actually have some news for her." PC Sansing doesn't explain what he means.

"Shall we all go and find her?" Mrs Sense suggests. "I'd like to offer her a bed for a few nights at least."

"Yes, we can all go in my car," PC Sansing says. "Your offer might not be necessary, but we'll see."

They pile into the police car as some curious neighbours have started wandering over to them from their houses. Not much happens in the sleepy village of Hadico so this street meeting is quite unusual. PC Sansing drives them as near as they can get to the field where Joseph's family have been staying. They all jump out and Joseph leads them into the wood and towards the edge of the field.

When they arrive, Joseph's mum is drying clothes on a line that she has put up between two trees. She looks tired and possibly ill.

"Hello, Mrs Kline," PC Sansing speaks to her and she jumps as she hadn't seen them approaching.

"Hi officer, is there a problem?" she says this automatically and then she sees Joseph, Reuben and Mrs Sense following behind. Mrs Kline stares at her son and then the others. She doesn't know quite what to say.

"No problem, are you the wife of Patrick Kline born in March 1956?" PC Sansing needs to be a little formal as he has important business to sort out.

"Yes, but my husband left us," she looks at Joseph as she says this.

"Maybe we should talk in private?" PC Sansing asks her.

"No, it's okay. It's probably time Joe knows the truth about his father." Mrs Kline turns to Joseph. "I didn't tell you this because I wanted to protect you. Your father didn't actually leave, he had to go to prison, he made some bad mistakes and lost all of our money. They gave him three months in prison and a very big fine. That's why we lost everything." Mrs Kline says it all in one breath and then waits for Joseph's reaction.

Joseph is in shock. He doesn't know whether to believe it or not. "So, why are you here then, officer?" He figures that the policeman has some news about his father.

"Your husband is staying at a local farm with a Mr and Mrs Jack. He was released from prison last month and has been searching for you ever since. From what the Jack's are saying, there have been some big changes in his life. He's been going to church with them I think." PC Sansing hopes that this is good news. He sees Mrs Kline's face light up when she hears that her husband is out of prison but then she looks sad again.

"I don't know what to say. Thank-you officer," she says.

"Would you like to see him? I can call the Jacks' and take you over there? What about you Joseph?" PC Sansing wants to be helpful.

"It's up to my mum." Joseph is very loyal and doesn't want to upset his mum but he has been missing his dad. He still can't really believe that they haven't been abandoned as he had thought.

"Yes, I think we should go," Mrs Kline says carefully. "I need to wake Jessica my youngest first, she's in there." She points to the tent.

Go to 83.

100.

The boys arrive back with Mrs Jessop. Mrs Sense thanks her neighbour and then heads back out with Reuben and Joseph behind her. The boys lead the way to where Joseph's family have been living. When they arrive, Joseph's mum is outside cleaning clothes in a basin of water. She jumps up when she sees them.

"Oh, Joe, who's this with you?" She looks at Mrs Sense.

"My son Reuben told me there were some people living here. I wanted to check you were okay," Mrs Sense says quickly before either of the boys can say anything.

"We are fine. We won't be here for long," Mrs Kline says but she doesn't look very well. "I think we might have had some bad water though as I've had a headache and my daughter Jess has been sick."

Mrs Sense is desperate to help them. "I don't want to embarrass you but there is plenty of space at our house and we would love to have you join us until you can get things sorted out." She waits as her offer sinks in.

"We are really okay," Mrs Kline says but she looks as if she might be tempted.

"How about just until you are feeling better? You can have a hot bath, some good food and a comfortable bed...." She hopes the offer sounds appealing.

"Well, maybe, but what about our stuff?" Mrs Kline starts thinking practically.

"We can carry it with us. Reuben and Joseph can take some of it and I can help. You must've got it here yourselves so I'm sure we can manage it." Mrs Sense is relieved that she has convinced the other woman.

They gather all of the belongings and take down the tent then head back to the Sense family home.

Go to 41.

101.

Mr and Mrs Sense are keenly waiting for an update when Mr Jack, Reuben and Ellie arrive back at the house. Mrs Sense told her husband all of the details as soon as he arrived back from work. He wants to help the family in the tent as much as she does, but they also want to take their time and make wise decisions.

Mr Jack asks if he can borrow their phone. He needs to call his wife. Reuben knows it is a bit naughty but he hangs around and tries to listen to the private phone call.

"Hi love, I think I may have found the other half of the Kline family. They are living in a tent on our land. He did tell us it was two kids, Joe and Jess, right?" Mr Jack wants to confirm the details before he does anything else.

"Yes, wife and two kids, Joe is eight and Jess four. Have you seen them then? How are they coping in the tent? What will you do?" Mrs Jack has a lot of questions. "I'm so glad you found them. I think we should tell Patrick that we've found them. At least then he won't need to keep going out searching. What do you think?"

"Slow down a second. Yes, I've met them, they seem to be doing okay but the lady looks a bit unwell. Yes, you can at least tell Patrick. I think the best thing for me to do is to explain everything to the Sense family as they are already involved. They might be able to take the three of them in, at least for a few weeks." Mr Jack feels sure that the Sense's will be willing to help.

He hangs up the phone and prepares to explain everything to them. They all sit round the big kitchen table. Reuben is included and he feels very important.

"Right, I think God may be working in this situation to bring a family back together. We will all need to play our part though. Shall we pray first?" Mr Jack knows the Sense's are Christians even though they attend a different church. That's one of the main reasons he feels sure they will help if they can.

They all bow their heads as the big farmer says a brief prayer asking for guidance and direction. Then he looks up and starts his story.

"About a month ago, I found a man sleeping on my land. He had been drinking and was miserable as he didn't have anywhere else to go. He told me a long story about losing his business after making some mistakes. He was sent to prison and his family lost their house. He was released from prison after just a few months and has been looking for his family but no one seems to know where they are. He heard a rumour that they had headed over this way which is why he came here. After chatting with the man a few times and talking to my wife, we decided to take him in for a while. We checked with the police and they confirmed that he had recently been released from prison for fraud." Mr Jack pauses for breath. Everyone is waiting for him to continue although they think they have guessed the rest of the story.

"Patrick Kline moved in with us and has been coming to our church. He has also been helping me on the farm. Just a week ago he became a Christian and started making some major changes in his life. He is determined to find his family and start again if they are willing," Mr Jack finishes and they all look at him.

"So, the people in the tent are the wife and children of the man living in your house!?" Mr Sense asks the obvious.

"Oh! Sorry, yes, I forgot the most important part of the story. They have the same name. It's definitely them." Mr Jack looks tired.

"But Joseph told me his dad left them and his mum also said that to you, Mr Jack. She didn't say anything about prison." Reuben feels like a detective trying to solve a crime as he puts the pieces together.

"Yes, I know. I think she was probably ashamed and didn't want the children to know if possible." Mr Jack guesses the reason for the lie.

"Now, I understand why you couldn't let them stay with you, Mr Jack. I'm sorry I kept asking." Reuben wishes he had trusted the big farmer.

"Well, there is only one thing to be done. We should have them here until they can find a new place to live," Mrs Sense says immediately and Mr Sense nods.

"That seems like a good plan as they might need some space to work this out especially as Mr Kline has become a Christian. That's really amazing," Mr Sense says.

"I hope his wife feels the same way, she didn't seem to want anything to do with religion," Mr Jack says.

"We can keep praying about that," Reuben adds.

Mrs Sense turns to Reuben. "If we have them here, Reuben, you will have to share your room and your things with Joseph. How do you feel about that?"

101Q. What will Reuben say?

A. "Let's leave them in the tent." <u>Go to 110</u>.

B. "I think it will be okay for a while. They need our help." <u>Go to 114</u>.

C. "I will put labels on all of my things so Joseph doesn't touch them." <u>Go to 72</u>.

102.

Reuben knows that he can't win every game. He finds it hard to lose but tries to be a good sport. He congratulates Joseph on his win. Joseph smiles and moves on to another game. Reuben sits down and watches him for a while. He hopes Joseph isn't going to take over and end up with more friends than he has!

As Reuben watches Joseph, he notices that he keeps looking behind him towards a hedge that runs alongside their garden. Joseph starts to move towards the hedge and away from the other people. The hedge appears to be moving and looks a bit strange. It's as if something or someone is hiding in it! Reuben sees a flash of blue as he continues watching. Joseph is now very close to the hedge and seems to be talking to whoever is in there.

Reuben starts to walk over to the area. He keeps his eyes focused on the hedge. There's definitely a person in there and the shape is too big to be a child. He can see a man's head now. He runs to tell his mum.

"Mum, Mum, I think there's a man in the hedge talking to Joseph," he shouts into the house.

"What? What are you talking about?" Mrs Sense appears and tries to understand what Reuben is saying.

"Come, quickly." Reuben drags her outside to the area and she immediately sees what Reuben is talking about. There is a man trying, not very successfully, to hide in their hedge!

Mrs Sense is very worried. She walks straight over to the man knowing that there are plenty of adults around if she needs them. "Can I help you? Who are you talking to Joseph?"

Joseph jumps and looks around. Everyone turns to look at him. The hedge stops moving but the man can clearly be seen now that people are moving closer. He climbs out and stands up straight. "Um, hi. I'm Joseph's father."

Everyone is stunned for a moment. "What were you doing in the hedge? You could've just come to the party, all parents were invited as well!" Mrs Sense doesn't want people to think that anyone was excluded from the party.

Joseph is still standing still as if he is in shock and doesn't know what to say. He had thought his dad had left their family but now he is being told something very different.

"I'm sorry for arriving like this, I didn't want to embarrass Joseph and I wasn't sure if he would want me to be here." Mr Kline looks around at everyone. "Great party," he adds.

"So, you didn't leave us by choice?" Joseph has found his voice.

"No, I'm so sorry, I did make some very bad mistakes and ended up in prison for a few months. A kind farmer took me in when I was released as I was sleeping in his field," Mr Kline explains. Looking around at the people at this party, he realises that they have probably never met anyone that has even slept in a field before. They definitely don't mix with people that have spent time in prison. Some people look uncomfortable and there is silence.

Mr Sense comes over to join his wife. "It's great to meet you. What did you say your name was?" He shakes the man's hand.

"Patrick, Patrick Kline." The man looks relieved not to have been kicked out of the party.

"So, you've been staying at the Jacks' farm?" Mr Sense assumes this as Mr Jack owns most of the land in the area and he has been known to take strangers in before.

"Yes, that's right, the Jack's." Mr Kline is happy that his story is starting to sound believable. He knows that hiding in a hedge probably wasn't the best idea. He is covered in bits of hedge and looks a bit like a tramp or a scarecrow.

"Come inside Mr Kline, let's have a cup of tea and then we can work out what to do next." Mr Sense is friendly.

Go to 109.

103.

Reuben bursts into tears. He grabs one of the hoops and throws it at Joseph. He stomps off into the house shouting, "It's my party, I wanted to win."

All of the guests are quiet and stare after him. Joseph wishes he had let Reuben win. He knows he has lost the chance to be his friend.

Mrs Sense follows Reuben into the house. "Reuben, how dare you behave like that?" She catches up to him. "How do you think Joseph feels? You can't win every game. You have to learn how to behave properly. You have so much to be thankful for."

"No, Mum. It's my party. I want to win

everything. I wish I hadn't invited him." Reuben throws himself down on the floor crying.

Hmm..this isn't likely to end well. Mr Sense will come in soon and will be furious. Mrs Sense is already angry. They will discipline Reuben who will miss the rest of his party. Reuben has also hurt God with his bad behaviour and he has shown all of his classmates and their parents a bad example of a Christian. Let's <u>go back to 85Q</u> and make a different choice, shall we?

104.

Reuben thinks quickly. He knows he cannot make a scene but he can embarrass Joseph in another way.

"Did you bring me a present, Joseph? Can I open it now?" Reuben says this in a loud voice knowing that Joseph has arrived empty handed and probably couldn't afford to bring a present.

Joseph looks down and as if he might cry. Everyone stares at him. "Reuben, I'm really sorry, I didn't bring you a gift. I didn't have enough money. I thought you wouldn't mind," he says.

Reuben feels terrible but is still angry that Joseph beat him in the game. "Oh, you should've bought me *something*," he says.

Mrs Sense has come into the garden and

overhears part of the conversation. She looks stunned. "Reuben, come inside right now. I'm ashamed of you. That's very nasty. You will go to bed and miss the rest of your party."

Oh! That's even worse than being a bad loser. Reuben has said something very mean that hurt Joseph a lot. It's definitely not something a Christian boy should have said. God is also hurt and Reuben will be disciplined by his parents. In fact, this unkindness is so serious that Reuben can't continue this book and will have to start again if he wants to know what happens. <u>Go to 1.</u>

105.

Reuben knows how to handle dogs. He has Dodgy at home. This is a smaller dog so he feels sure that he can deal with it. He tries to grab hold of the yapping dog and carry it away with him. The dog thinks it's a great game and snaps and bites him playfully.

"Ouch, owwwww," Reuben yells as the dog sinks its teeth into the flesh on his arm. It has let go of his trouser leg though so Reuben manages to pick it up. He tries to ignore the pain as he heads out of the front door with the dog still hanging onto his arm.

He can hear the old couple yelling, "Stop,

thief. That's our dog. What are you doing?"

Reuben stops. He is halfway down the drive. The shouts of the adults have woken him up. What is he doing? Breaking into the house was an innocent mistake as he had really believed that Joseph lived here but now he is stealing a dog! That isn't a mistake.

He puts the dog down. It finally lets go of his arm and grabs his trouser leg again. Reuben walks back towards the house to speak to the old people.

Go to 106.

106.

"I can explain everything," Reuben shouts as the old man comes towards him. He wants to check his injuries but realises that will have to wait.

"You'd better do it quickly," the man says. He looks grim.

"I'm so sorry. My friend told me he lived here. We found the hidden key outside and went in through the back door. We haven't taken anything. It's the truth, honestly." Reuben is sobbing. He is really scared.

"How old are you? You only look about seven!" The man is closer now and can see that he is dealing with a small boy who looks afraid.

"I'm eight, I live in the village. I think I've been to visit you before with my family." Reuben adds this hoping it will make him seem more believable

"What's your second name?" the man demands.

"I'm Reuben Sense," he says nervously.

"The Sense's boy. Yes, you did come here once. How did you get yourself mixed up in this?" The man is surprised and is starting to believe Reuben's story even though it sounded crazy at first.

"So, who is the boy that was with you?" he asks.

"His name's Joseph. He just started at my school. I think this is all my fault as I kept asking if I could go to his house and I think he felt he had to say yes. Maybe his house is very small and he didn't want me to see it." Reuben is starting to put the pieces together.

"Nothing's missing." The lady joins them. She has been listening in the background whilst checking everything.

"Okay, let's get you home. I think I will take you myself. You can stop crying now." The man is stern but gentle as he realises what has happened.

The man takes Reuben home and tells

Reuben's horrified parents what has happened. The old man asks them not to be too tough on him.

Reuben tells his parents that Joseph has run away and tells them everything he knows about him so far, which isn't much. Joseph doesn't return to school. He has left the area.

Reuben must've scared Joseph away by being too keen to see his house before he was ready. Let's go back to 32Q at Reuben's house when Joseph is about to leave after his visit and make a different decision.

107.

Reuben is good at making up stories as he's read so many Enid Blyton books.

"Your dog escaped into the road outside. I was just walking past and I saw it and wanted to put it back inside for you." Reuben waits to see what the man makes of his lie.

"That's an interesting story, young man. How did you get into our house?" The man doesn't look like he believes Reuben's story.

"I searched and found the spare key," Reuben says.

"Really, and you think that's okay, do you? Breaking into our house. I don't believe you.

Chappy was locked in. If you found him in the street then how did you know which house he was from?" The man is trying to catch Reuben out.

Reuben glances down at the dog and sees that he has a tag around his neck. "I read it on his tag," he says quickly.

"Oh dear, the tag only has a phone number….." The man knows that he has won the battle.

"I mean, I remember seeing the dog with you in the village before," Reuben says.

"We don't take Chappy into the village." The man is moving towards Reuben

This is a ridiculous situation. Reuben isn't sure whether he even believes his lies anymore. The man certainly doesn't! Let's tell the man the truth instead, shall we?

Go to 106.

108.

Reuben is still shocked but realises that Joseph needs his help. "Okay, just be as quick as you can," he says.

Joseph disappears into the woods. Joseph's dad doesn't try to follow him, he just waits. "So, you are in Joe's class at school?" he asks.

"Yes, but we don't know each other that well as he's only just started," Reuben explains.

"Well, thankyou anyway for being friends with Joe, everything that has happened isn't his fault. It's mine." Joseph's father looks broken and Reuben feels sorry for him.

After about ten minutes, Reuben hears the noises of someone coming towards them. It's Joseph….and his mum!

The two adults obviously have a lot of talking to do, but they can't really do it with the boys there. Reuben senses this and says, "Joseph, I think we should go back to my house whilst your parents talk to each other. Is that okay?"

Joseph's mother and father look relieved. "Yes, that would be really helpful, Joe, can you go with him?" Joseph's mother says.

After giving the adults an address, the two boys set off for Reuben's house leaving Joseph's parents to talk.

Reuben explains everything to his parents when they arrive back at his house.

Several hours later, Joseph's parents also arrive at the house. They are smiling but both have red eyes. The Sense family welcome them in and Mrs Sense puts food in front of them. She invites Mrs Kline and Joseph to stay until the family can work out where they will be living. Mr Kline will return to the Jacks' house as they still need some time to talk about what went wrong.

After a week or so, the government manages to rehouse the family in the area. Mr and Mrs Kline and their children move into their new home. Mr Kline persuades his family to go to church with him. He is encouraged that the Sense family are Christians as well. Mrs Kline and Joseph also realise that they are surrounded by Christians who have been helping them. They listen carefully to the messages at church.

Reuben prays that they will soon understand the truth of the Christian message. He is grateful to have a true friend in Joseph. He has learned a lot about caring for others and sharing the things that he has.

Go to 111.

109.

Mr Sense calls Mr Jack on the phone and asks him to come over and join them. He sits down with Mr Kline in their kitchen. "I've asked Mr Jack to come over, do you mind if I pray first before we talk?" he asks.

"Please do," Mr Kline responds and bows his head.

When Mr Jack arrives, they have a long chat.

Mr Sense believes that Mr Kline is really a changed man. He has been attending church with the Jack's and seems to want to sort things out.

"I want to help you. I know that sometimes we all need a new start," Mr Sense reassures him. "Shall we get Reuben and Joseph here to see if we can get the whole story together?"

They call the boys to join them and work out the missing details of the last few months. Mr Kline is horrified to find out that his family have been living in a tent due to him being unable to provide for them.

After a while, they decide that it would be best if Mrs Kline and the children stay with the Sense family. Mr Kline will continue to live with the Jack's until they have had a chance to talk things through. Mr Kline decides he will go back to the farm straight away as he knows that his wife will need some space and time to think things through when she finds out that he is in the area.

Mrs Sense wants to talk to Reuben alone first though. "Reuben, you know that if they come to stay with us, you will have to share a room, and your things, with Joseph?

109Q. What will Reuben say?
A. "Let's leave them in the tent." <u>*Go to 110*</u>.

B. "I think it will be okay for a while. They need our help." <u>Go to 114.</u>

C. "I will put labels on all of my things so Joseph doesn't touch them." <u>Go to 72.</u>

110.

Really!? After coming all this way and taking all this time to investigate Joseph's situation. Reuben wants to leave them in the tent just so he can keep his bedroom and his things to himself? That's pretty selfish, don't you think? Let's <u>go back to 101Q</u> and rethink this decision.

111.

If Reuben has reached this far in the story, I'm sure he has learned a lot of important lessons.

Joseph is from a family that ended up living in a tent with little money and few things. His dad had spent time in prison having been convicted of a crime. The family had been separated.

Reuben has all the things he could wish for and more. He has a mum and dad with a happy marriage. He has friends at school and in the area. He is popular.

The main difference, though, between Reuben's family and Joseph's is that Reuben is from a Christian family and Joseph isn't. As far as we can tell Joseph's family have had no interest in God until nearer the end of the story. This means that Reuben's friendship with Joseph could be very important.

What if God brought Joseph into Reuben's life so that Reuben could show him how a real Christian behaves? Has Reuben been careful to show love and care in the way that a Christian should as he has made his decisions?

The Bible says in Hebrews 13 vs 16:

"Do not neglect to do good and to share what you have, for such sacrifices are pleasing to God."

And in Matthew 5 vs 42:

"Give to the one who begs from you, and do not refuse the one who would borrow from you."

There are a lot of other Bible verses about caring for others and sharing what we have. We need to remember where our money and things came from in the first place.

"Every good gift and every perfect gift is from above, coming down from the Father of lights." (James 1 vs 17.)

So, all of our blessings are from God. God

wants us to share them with others. When we do this we are showing them that God cares for them as well. Let's try to be good witnesses for God here on earth.

THE END.

112.

"Oh, hello, Sir. I'm sorry to be in your hedge! My friend told me he lives at this house, but now I think that maybe he wasn't telling the truth. Please, can you stop your dog from biting me." Reuben calms down a little as the man doesn't seem angry, he just looks surprised that his hedge is now talking to him.

"What? Who is that? Come out, please. Chappy leave it, come here." The man calls his dog and Reuben emerges from the hedge.

"So, there are two of you? Where is your friend then?" the man asks.

Reuben decides to leave Joseph out of it. "I'm not sure Sir, maybe he left already."

"No, it's okay Reuben, I'm still here." Joseph climbs out of the hedge and stands beside Reuben. "I'm sorry Sir, this is my fault. I actually live in a tent right now and I didn't want my friend to know because he is rich and has a big house. I saw that your house was empty so I pretended it was mine." Joseph owns up.

Reuben feels terrible. He hadn't realised that this might happen if he insisted on seeing Joseph's house. A lot of things are starting to add up now. "You're living in a tent?" he asks Joseph.

"Why?" the man joins in with questions.

"It's just for a while. My dad left when he lost all our money," Joseph admits.

"I wish you had told me. I'm sure my family would be able to help," Reuben offers.

"Yes, I should've just told you," Joseph says.

"Right, boys, I think I'm going to take you home and then you can sort this out. Next time, please don't hide in an old man's hedge as you might give him a heart-attack!" The man laughs. He waits for the two boys as they collect Reuben's books and then the three of them walk to Reuben's house.

The old man drops the boys off safely and after a brief word with Mrs Sense he leaves them to explain the rest.

On hearing the whole story, Mrs Sense, of course, wants to meet Joseph's mum to see if she can do anything to help. She asks the boys to call on Mrs Jessop, a neighbour, to ask her to come over and watch the other kids for her. Whilst they are gone she calls Mr Sense to make sure her plan

is okay with him.
Go to 100.

113.

Reuben wishes he had realised how much he would be taking on when he tried to befriend Joseph. He sees his chance to escape and takes it. "I'm sorry, I must get home or I'll be in trouble," he mumbles. He knows that his mum wouldn't mind him being out if she knew the circumstances but he doesn't really want to be this involved in Joseph's life. He rushes off before anyone can argue with him!

After that day, Reuben sees Joseph around at school but Joseph doesn't really talk to him. His clothes look a bit tidier and he is cleaner. Reuben guesses that his family must have sorted things out and found a place to live now. Other children in the class become friends with Joseph but Reuben sticks to his own friends.

It's really such a shame that Reuben didn't take his opportunity to show Christian kindness to Joseph and his family. Others may have helped them now or the government may have given them somewhere to live, but Reuben had the chance to show them that God loves them and he didn't take it because their problems seemed too complicated. I wonder what he would do if he <u>*went back to 91Q*</u> *and made his last decision again?*

114.

Although Reuben doesn't much like the thought of having to share everything. He knows what he needs to do. He knows Joseph's family need help for a while. "Let's try to help them," he says.

"I'll stay here with Noah and Toby. You go and meet Mrs Kline," Mr Sense suggests to his wife.

Mr Jack, Mrs Sense, Reuben and Ellie head out to go and talk to the half of the Kline family living in the pink tent.

When they arrive, Mrs Kline is hand washing clothes in a bowl outside the tent. She looks up and seems surprised to see everyone.

"I heard that you were out here and hadn't been feeling that well. I wondered if we could help, just until you are feeling better? We just live nearby." Mrs Sense knows that she has only just met the other lady and doesn't want to push her.

"We are fine. We won't be here for long" Mrs Kline says but she doesn't look very well. "I think we might have had some bad water though as I've had a headache and my daughter Jess has been sick."

Mrs Sense is desperate to help them. "I don't want to embarrass you but there is plenty of space at our house and we would love to have you join us until you can get things sorted out." She waits as her offer sinks in.

"We are really okay," Mrs Kline says but she looks as if she might be tempted.

"How about just until you are feeling better. You can have a hot bath, some good food and a comfortable bed." Mrs Sense hopes the offer sounds appealing.

"Well, maybe. But what about our stuff?" Mrs Kline starts thinking practically.

"We can carry it with us. Reuben and Joseph can take some and I can help. You must've got it here yourselves so I'm sure we can manage it." Mrs Sense is relieved that she has convinced the other woman.

They gather all of the belongings and take down the tent then head back to the Sense family home.

Mr Jack heads home for the time being as he knows that it is not yet time to discuss Mrs Kline's husband with her.

Go to 95.